FACES OF DECEPTION

By Elizabeth Parker

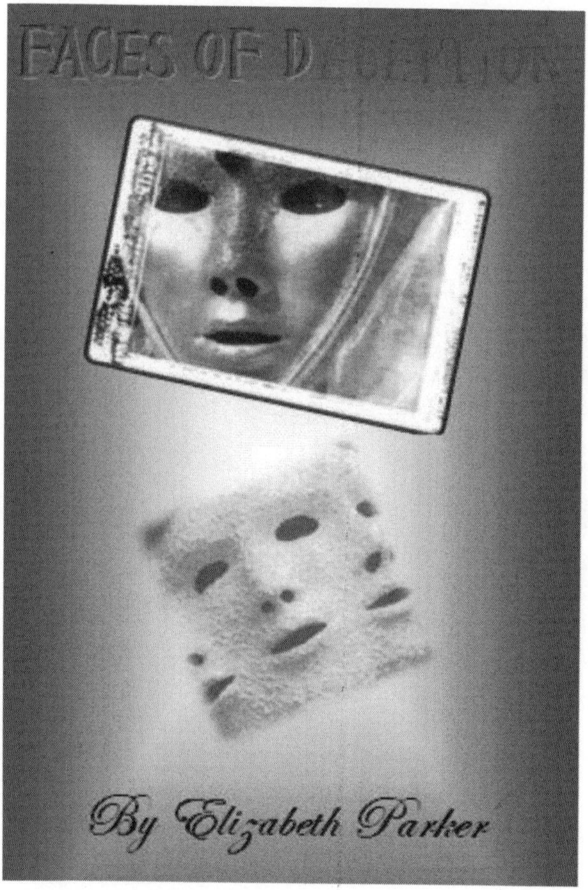

Copyrighted Material
Copyrighted © 2012 Elizabeth Parker

All rights reserved. No part of this publication may be reproduced or transmitted in any form by any means, electronic or mechanical, including photocopy, recording, or any information storage and retrieval system, without permission in writing from the publisher.

Faces of Deception is a work of fiction. Names, characters, places and incidents are the product of the author's imagination. Any resemblance to actual persons, living or dead, or events is entirely coincidental.

First Edition

ISBN 10: 1466346299
ISBN-13: 978-1466346291

To order this book or if you have any questions or comments, please visit me at
www.elizabethparkerbooks.com

A portion of the proceeds from the sales of this book will be donated to an animal rescue group.

To My Husband- Thanks for always being there and especially for causing me to have uncontrollable laughing fits.

Brandi, Toffee and Buddy Junior - Always remain as silly as you are. You are all wonderful.

Mom, we seriously need to find new words for scrabble, but I'm glad we found Qi.

    ***

For Buddy- You'll always be our ray of sunshine. We think about you every day and miss you more as time passes. Save us all a spot at the rainbow bridge.

Chapter 1: False Accusations?

"I know it was you, Montgomery. So help me if I find out that I'm right." Carmine slammed his fist on the counter hard enough to cause the dusty cash register to bounce.

The shop had that musty odor that signified a professional cleaning crew had never stepped foot on premises.

"Boss, I'm telling you. It wasn't me. Why would I steal from you? Huh? Tell me that. I've been working here too long for me to take anything from you and Donovan. I swear! You have my word."

"Who else would've done it? The mice?" He raised his voice, causing his face to turn lobster-red and his eyes to transform into tiny slits. "Oh, I know. Maybe a mouse gently opened the front door without any signs of forced entry—perhaps they had an imaginary key—and stole money right out of the cash register and then quietly walked out. Sure! That makes tons of sense. Why didn't I think of that earlier? Then, that same rodent came back again and again, and not only stole money, but almost every expensive tool that we own. Is *that* what happened, Montgomery? You lanky lowlife!"

"No, I—I don't know what happened. But, I'll find out for you. I promise, I would never do anything like that. It wasn't me."

"Oh, well thank goodness we cleared that up. That's great!" Carmine was infamous for being facetious. "You have a week to find out who is responsible. I'll break your legs if I find out it was you. Don't test me. You know I will."

Ordinarily, Montgomery was an arrogant one. He looked like he belonged in a '50s street gang, with his black hair slicked back and his smokes rolled up in his T-shirt. But he had the skills of a good plumber when he wasn't high on cocaine, and that was the only reason he kept his job.

He was a little intimidated as Carmine's veins pulsed on his forehead. They resembled bulging egg sacks that might hatch little aliens from them any minute. "If it was you, you better run and run far. I've taken enough of your horseshit throughout the years, but this is my breaking point. Do you hear me?" He threw a coffee can filled with nails at Montgomery's head, purposely missing him by a quarter of an inch. "Next time, I'll aim directly for your head and I won't miss. That, I can assure you. Donovan is going through the videotapes and if I see your sorry ass on there, you're dead."

"You're wrong, boss. It wasn't me. I don't know what I can do to prove it to ya, but I'm telling you, you're wrong!"

"Fantastic. Then I'll hire you back on Monday and maybe even apologize, but something tells me I won't be doing any of that! If it was you, you won't need a job where you're going. Take my advice and watch your back, son. You'd better learn how to grow eyes in the back of your head. Now get the hell out of here."

Carmine, the co-owner of South Side Plumbing for which Montgomery worked, always came across as though he'd been served vinegar with a side of lemons as his morning's breakfast, even when not accusing his employees of stealing. It was rare to see a smile on his face, and if you did, it was most likely because he had a piece of food lodged between his yellowing teeth.

And though functional and sometimes even profitable, the plumbing business was just a facade.

Once, Carmine had actually made a modest living as a rookie plumber, who only dabbled in the drug scene every once in a while. But as with many drug users, his priorities in life shifted, turning his life of dabbling into a dependency.

Unable to handle the day-to-day responsibility of reporting to a higher authority, he partnered with Donovan, another drug user, though not yet an addict, to start their own company, though it was really a front. He needed to report his income somehow, even though a fraction of it came from dealing drugs. While the front of the shop looked normal, the backroom would be heaven to any drug addict lucky enough to stumble upon it. Upon first glance, it resembled a disorganized office. A wooden table covered with invoices stood in the middle of the room, the wood chipping off of both sides. Two metal chairs sat on either side of it, the kind that hurt to sit in after only a few minutes. To the left were a few shelves that held supplies—paper towels, pens, invoices, clipboards, and a few stray tools. What couldn't be seen without closer inspection were fireproof safes that were carefully hidden underneath the floorboards or neatly tucked in the walls behind secret wooden panels. These safes housed scrupulously-measured bags of cocaine separated by grams, along with marijuana, methamphetamine, ecstasy, oxycodone, and a myriad of other drugs.

As Montgomery walked out of the shop, Carmine shouted something behind him, no doubt some type of threat. But the door slammed before he could hear it. Montgomery knew Carmine would stop at nothing to get revenge—he'd done it before.

In the beginning of their joint venture, Donovan kept Carmine on his toes. Carmine and Donovan both worked full-time, but once Carmine's social use became more of an everyday necessity, his work ethic became only a vague memory. Donovan knew Carmine had a problem when he started using drugs more than he sold them. His violent temper was often piqued when he couldn't get his hands on a quick fix.

Though Donovan dabbled as well, he was at least able to exercise some self-control. He didn't depend upon drugs to get through his daily routine. Carmine, on the other hand, seemed to be losing his common sense with each passing day, so it was no wonder that he'd flown off the handle when his money disappeared, and then later that week when his tools vanished as well.

A rumor had it that Carmine had injured people for less than theft, though it was a rumor Montgomery believed with all of his heart.

Montgomery knew that if Donovan caught anything suspicious on the security tapes, Carmine would make good on his promise. He only hoped Donovan, known for his levelheadedness, would step in and talk some sense into his uncontrollable partner.

Chapter 2: 'Til Death Do Us Part

Tonight was going to be a superb evening for Montgomery. He and his friends had scored a deal on some cocaine and were having a party at Shelby's house. He and Shelby had started dating—if you could call it that—a few months prior. Their *dates* consisted of getting high on whatever drugs fell into their possession.

All of the cool people were going to be there. Artie, their main source, hinted that he was bringing along some ecstasy as well, and there was no way that Montgomery was missing it.

Just like Carmine and Donovan, Montgomery also frequented the drug scene. It hadn't gotten to the point where his incessant need for drugs surpassed his ability to hold down a job, but he was definitely traveling steadily on the path toward addiction, similar to his parents. He used his upbringing as an excuse to do whatever he wanted, whenever he wanted.

His father, Brian Allen Vendora, was a raging alcoholic who had never encountered a bottle he didn't like. There was no way in hell *he* could ever hold down a job, and he frequently took out his frustrations on his wife, as well as Montgomery, and his older brother, Lewis.

His parents fought day in and day out. It wasn't just tiny squabbles—their fights made televised boxing look like a sophisticated night at the ballet. Even as his mother's face met the end of his father's fist again and again, she clung to the old-fashioned theory that she should never leave, no matter how unbearable her life became.

Perhaps she *couldn't* leave. Her suitcases were occasionally packed and lined up by the doorway, but somehow, some way, Mr. Vendora always discovered that his wife was planning on going on a permanent vacation—

without him. And when he did, Mrs. Vendora wouldn't be seen for days on end.

He saw his actions as punishment for her indecent behavior, and after a while, she succumbed to the old cliché—if you can't beat him, join him. She started to indulge in more and more liquid meals herself. The two of them found solace in sharing a bottle of bourbon whiskey. From a distance, one might assume that Cupid had arranged the perfect match.

But Montgomery knew his mother drank to expedite her inevitable death, having decided it was impossible to make a clean getaway during in life. He questioned her poor choices and wondered why she never sought help.

Plus, the more inebriated that she became, the less she cared when her husband beat their kids to a pulp. During her sober days, she'd step in and take the brunt to protect her children, but that came to a halt when the tipped bottle became more important.

By the time Montgomery was fourteen, he had begun to scout out places where he could sleep overnight, especially during his parents' drinking binges. They were usually too far gone to notice him leave, and by the time morning rolled around, he always returned with his parents none the wiser.

The next year, his father's abuse landed his brother Lewis in the hospital, with bruises covering a good portion of his face and body. Once Lewis recovered, both boys left home to stay with friends. Lewis found a job first and then helped Montgomery get hired.

As bad as their childhoods were, once they were on their own, they were both surprisingly responsible. They found a small one-bedroom apartment on the south side of town, which they shared and split the rent. Lewis gave the bedroom to Montgomery, while he slept in the center of the tiny living room.

Lewis worked hard to pick up the pieces of his life, consciously refraining from alcohol and drugs. But Montgomery eventually gave in to his own self-pity and spent his free time drinking and partying like there was no tomorrow. He told Lewis that he had "earned that right." It was only a matter of time before he began to experiment with marijuana, and then graduated to a few lines of cocaine here and there. After two years on his own, Montgomery was experimenting with heroin and any other street drugs he could get his hands on. It was a wonder that he was still able to keep a job, but he knew that in order to get his hands on drugs, he needed to work.

One night, after a full day of partying, Montgomery stumbled into the apartment that he shared with Lewis, breaking a lamp and waking his brother in the process. When Lewis told him that he had had enough and demanded that Montgomery get his life together, Montgomery began screaming in a petulant rage. He took a swing at Lewis, missed, and fell face down on the floor.

That was the end of the proverbial rope for Lewis. While he didn't want to be responsible for tying the noose, he didn't want to be an enabler, either. He had lived his entire childhood witnessing alcoholism and abuse. He didn't want to stand by to see his brother spiral out of control.

Left with no other choice, he packed his brother's bags and gave him until the end of the week to get out, hoping it would be the motivation that his brother needed to get his life in order.

Unfortunately, it had the adverse effect, because Montgomery, then age seventeen, left the next morning without saying a word. From that point on, he rented rooms from people, lived with strangers that he met on the street, and sometimes, his home was nothing more than a cardboard box or a rusty, cold bench in the middle of a vacant park. He hadn't seen his brother since.

He never regretted his choice to cut ties —or at least he never let on if he did—and never tried to contact Lewis again. When he acquired employment with Carmine three years later, he admitted that he considered his brother dead.

Chapter 3: Idle Threats

"Hey Carmine, there's nothing in those damn tapes. Not a damn thing!"

"What the hell do you mean, Don? How could you be so naive? You know damn well that it was Montgomery behind all of this. You always have a soft spot for that punk. I say we give him what he deserves. We got this supposedly kick-ass video security system and it didn't even catch the guy? The freaking camera is right above the cash register. How could it *not* catch him?"

"Calm down and just shut up for one minute, will you? If you'd stop running your mouth and just listen for thirty seconds, maybe you'd understand what I have to say." Carmine started to get up to flex his muscles but quickly sat back down. Even he knew his limits. Though Carmine was a big guy, Donovan was bigger. A fight between the two of them wouldn't be pretty, and Carmine's face would leave a permanent indentation in the ground. Carmine kept quiet long enough for Donovan to continue. "Listen closely. It caught the guy, Carmine, but the person in this video was not stupid. He was not an amateur. He was clever enough to wear a mask and gloves. He—or she—also has on a black coat, which is not that odd, since it was cold that day. I'd love to tell you it was Montgomery, but there's just no proof. You can watch it for yourself if you don't believe me."

Fuming inside, Carmine wanted to lash out at Donovan. Regardless if it was Montgomery, he needed that money for a fix and now it was gone. Any funds they had made this past week were for the shop. He thought about stealing from his buyers' stash, but that would be the worst thing he could do.

Sadly enough, Donovan had to control the finances and write out the checks for Carmine's mortgage each month before giving Carmine anything leftover from his paycheck—a deal they made during one of Carmine's sober moments, when they realized Carmine was not responsible enough to pay his bills before paying for his drugs.

"So, what do you want to do about it, Carmine? You still want to fire the guy?"

"I don't know. I know he's up to something. I can feel it."

"Well, until your psychic abilities start proving themselves, we have nothing to go on." His sarcasm was all but lost on his partner, but for Donovan, it was time to put Carmine in his place. "Regardless of the fact that you don't have any love for the guy, Montgomery is a decent worker. He shows up on time, give or take fifteen minutes, and gets the job done. Our clients like him and in case you forgot, we've got a legitimate business to run." Carmine listened, the steam still protruding from his ears. "On a personal level, Monty's brought you a good share of pills and powder when you were down on your luck. Let's not forget he's helped *you* party more times than I'd personally like to admit."

"You know, Don, you act so pristine, like you don't get high? You're just as guilty as I am."

"I never said that that I was pristine." Carmine was pouting like a child, his fist extending and retracting, exhibiting his nervous tic. "There comes a time though when you need to exercise *some* self-control. That's all I'm saying. You party like you're twenty years old. You're forty, man. Time to lose the temper, lose the addiction, and run our company. You can't accuse every Tom, Dick, and Harry of stealing from us." He paused to gauge his partner's reaction. When there wasn't one, he continued.

"Listen, before you go running your mouth off, I need you to sign these business and lease renewal forms. Just sign by the 'x.'"

"Yeah, yeah. Give me the damn papers. You got a pen?"

"Here, use this one." Distracting him now, he continued. "Carmine, I know it sucks that we got robbed. Believe me, though I may seem calm, cool, and collected, I'm pissed off beyond belief. Unfortunately, we're not in the best position ourselves. Do you want the cops to look around and see our drug paraphernalia in the backroom? Do you want someone to blow the whistle on us? I sure as hell don't. There's nothing we can do about it this time. If it happens again, we'll catch the son of a bitch. For now, sit tight. They didn't get everything. We'll batten down the hatches tighter next time."

"Yeah, I'll say. Get a freaking attack dog on the bastard."

"Yeah, sure, and you'll come in the store in a drunken stupor only to have him attack you. That'll go over real well."

Laughing to himself now at Carmine's foolish temper, Donovan stopped when his partner's face turned crimson. When Carmine got angry, his face resembled a red rocoto pepper, with the heated rage to match. Donovan wasn't in the frame of mind for another altercation. Carmine's mood swings were becoming more and more frequent.

"We got any more jobs today?" Carmine asked.

"Nope, just writing out the last of our bills and calling it a night. You can go home. I'll lock up."

"Fine, I'm outta here. See ya tomorrow."

Feeling defeated, Carmine got into his car. His gut told him Montgomery was guilty, but without his partner's consent, he couldn't fire him. The truth was, they needed Montgomery for the time being.

He hated being taken advantage of. He had come too far in life to have people stealing from him. If anyone had a right to extra money, it was him, not Montgomery.

"If he did it, he'll get caught," he said to himself as he sped away from the shop. "Everyone slips up eventually. And when he does, I'll be right there to kick him back down. Six feet down."

Chapter 4: Charmed Living

Once the moving company had unloaded all of the boxes and furniture into her new home, Jacqueline stood in the center of her living room for a moment to take it all in.

"This is all mine," she said to herself. "I did it without any help from anybody. Now the fun part. Unpacking."

It was April by the time Jacqueline had signed the rental agreement for the charming house in Suffolk County. The couple renting her the house had mentioned that they were looking to sell in a few years, and that if she liked it, they would offer it to her first.

She had lived with her parents for longer than she'd anticipated, but doing so had given her the time to save up enough money. Most of her friends were still sacrificing nights of divine freedom under the secure roofs of their parents.

Jacqueline got along beautifully with her own folks. Aside from a brief stage of teenage rebellion, she had had no issues with them. But at age twenty-three, she was ready to start living independently, which had been her dream since she was nineteen.

Jacqueline always followed through with her goals. She had a distinctive way about her on the whole. Though she was average in looks, she had the confidence of a seasoned movie star. Nothing was unattainable to her, and she had no qualms about making sacrifices along the way.

When she was younger, she had been terrified of swimming. The thought of even wading frightened her, since there didn't seem to be any plausible way that the buoyancy of the water would enable a human to float. Gravity would drag her body down into the depths of a dizzying whirlpool to a cavernous black hole, never to be discovered. She had convinced herself that stepping foot inside of a pool was like signing your own death certificate.

But at age thirteen, she became desperate to overcome her fear. Her parents thought swimming lessons were a waste of money, figuring her fear was so intense that Jacqueline would get cold feet or become restless and they would lose their deposit.

But she was determined to show her parents that that they were wrong, so Jacqueline saved money from holiday gifts and from helping out with small jobs around the neighborhood. By fourteen, she had saved enough money to pay for the lessons herself. It only took another year before she had shed her fears and become a decent swimmer. By eighteen, she was a respected lifeguard at the public beach.

Soon after, she surprised her parents again by obtaining a black belt in tae kwon do. They finally understood that there was nothing Jacqueline couldn't do if she put her mind to it. It was as if she were impervious to failure.

As with every fairytale, however, sometimes life's obstacles show up out of nowhere and can't be avoided.

She found this out the hard way when she got caught speeding in her new friend Shelby Winfred's car. Jacqueline was too young to have a license, although she did know how to drive, and figured it was safer with her behind the wheel rather than Shelby, who was intoxicated that night.

Jacqueline only later found out Shelby was more than drunk—she had been high on cocaine and a bouquet of similar drugs. She also found out that the car was not, in fact, Shelby's, but instead belonged to a Mr. Griego, who had reported his prized Mercedes stolen only a few hours earlier. When the police booked Jacqueline, they searched through her belongings and found a small bag of cocaine neatly stuffed toward the bottom of her purse, underneath her wallet—a convenient way for Shelby to resist getting arrested.

While Jacqueline was innocent of all charges, her incompetent lawyer couldn't support a case strong enough to prove it. Since she was a minor and had no prior arrests, she spent time in juvenile detention, and was let out on good behavior in less than six months' time—only now with the word "convict" stamped on her record in big, bold, red ink.

Once released, she never interacted with any of those "friends" again. She got her life back on track, thankful that she was actually able to get a job as a lifeguard over the summer, doing what she loved. Eventually she got a full-time job during the day and attended college in the evenings. She majored in advertising, which gave her the ability to exercise her creative side.

Any extra money that she earned was promptly put aside into a savings account. When she decided it was time to be on her own, she ensured that she had enough to cover rent for the first three months—less than the six months' advisers recommended.

Proud of her independence, she was determined to afford something a little bigger than an apartment, so she set her sights higher and looked in the classifieds for a house to rent.

From assembling a budget and sticking to it, to researching demographics and monthly expenses, to finding a more secure job than the one she had—one with the opportunity for advancement and frequent salary increases—Jacqueline's plan was meticulous and effective. When she was passionate about something, she made it happen.

Her new home was a small two-bedroom ranch-style house with a country setting, and the backyard even had a luxurious built-in pool that was hers to use when the weather was warm enough.

But it was the picturesque front yard that had captured her full attention and clutched at her heartstrings: a freshly-painted mid-size porch led to the front door and when in bloom, an array of colorful flowers and tiny shrubs beautified the front lawn. Since it was an exceptionally mild spring, tiny buds had started to form on the perennial plants, and they were ready to blossom any day now.

Since her morning had just begun and she had a lot of work to do, she opened all of the windows to let her new home air out. She was a certified neat freak, and a speck of dust could send her into frenzy, so the first order of business was to make sure that the house sparkled. The counter was cluttered with an assortment of cleaning supplies.

As she wiped down the countertops and cabinets, she envisioned the perfect place for each item and knickknack, storing mental notes to be retrieved once she was ready to unpack and decorate.

Toward noon, she took a moment to relax. Realizing she hadn't had anything to drink in quite a while, she poured herself a glass of raspberry iced tea and took a seat on top of the granite counter. She wrapped her slender fingers around the glass of tea and enjoyed the fresh air seeping in through the window.

Outside, a group of children played in the street. It was a friendly neighborhood and everyone in the community appeared happy and cordial. She had hoped to meet at least some of them by the end of the month and maybe even make a few friends.

Jacqueline finished her cold drink, letting the sweet liquid coat her parched throat. She took one last glance outside, caught eyes with a rather handsome neighbor, and managed a small wave. He waved back as she hopped off of the counter and out of sight.

She tied her long brown hair back from her face and exhaled. "Okay, enough of that," she said. "It's time to get back to work. Maybe later they'll be time to flirt," she added with a giggle.

By nightfall, Jacqueline's muscles were sore and her lower back felt like knotted rope. She had accomplished enough work for the day and deemed it mandatory to call it quits, even though there was still much to be done.

Her bed was centered in her bedroom, fully-made with brand-new sheets and a light comforter. A twelve-pack of soda was chilling in the fridge, along with a bottle of Boysenberry Dessert Wine.

Why not? I deserve it.

After popping the cork, she poured herself a glass and opened the box of chocolates that her father had given her.

Delicious. Chocolate and wine. The perfect ending to a productive day.

She tried to recall if she had thanked her father and elected to call him in the morning.

Since it was still warm outside, she stepped onto the porch of her new abode, set her wine glass down on the small table, and sat down on the canary-yellow chaise lounge. Before long, she had closed her eyes and let the soft breeze sweep her brow.

"Hi there!"

"Whoa! Oh, you scared me! I just closed my eyes for a minute."

Standing at the base of her porch was the same handsome man she had noticed earlier. She couldn't help but notice his thick dark hair, and that he had the most gorgeous blue eyes she had ever seen. When he smiled, his teeth were equally perfect.

"Sorry to startle you. I just wanted to introduce myself. My name's Benjamin, but please don't call me that." He flashed another charming smile. "You can call me Ben, or Benny. Just not Benjamin."

It was easy to tell he was nervous by his nonsensical chatter, but Jacqueline made him feel comfortable at once. "Hi, I'm Jacqueline, but you can call me Jackie. Just don't call me Jack."

She winked as she extended her hand, but noticed his eyes shift to her wine glass and then back toward her with a cheeky smirk.

"Oh, goodness," she said. "You must think I'm some sort of a drunk with my wine glass next to me, sleeping on the front porch." She waved her hand in front of her face. "I just moved in today and have been cleaning and unpacking since six o'clock this morning."

With a laugh, he interrupted. "No need to explain. It's okay that you're a wino. Come to think of it, I never met a wino that I didn't like."

She quickly realized he was teasing. "Well, on that note, there's more where this came from. Would you like a glass? I'm not inviting you in, so don't get any ideas, but I'm about to get myself a refill and don't want to appear rude."

A full grin was now painted on his face. "Sure, I'd love some, and just so *you* don't get any ideas, I'm not that type of guy anyway."

"Touché!" A moment later, Jacqueline reappeared on the porch. Ben was already sitting in the cushioned chair opposite hers. She liked him already. She couldn't help but feel she was sizing him up, but when she walked out, it seemed he was guilty of the same. "I hope you have a sweet tooth," she said. "It's a dessert wine, so it's very sugary, but very delicious. Here's some chocolate to go with it. Please eat some. While I'm not a wino, I *am* a recovering chocoholic so I will eat that entire box by myself if you don't help me out."

"Well, I can't possibly turn down a lady in distress now, can I?"

She shook her head and smiled coquettishly. "No, you cannot."

"So, just moving in, huh? Where are you from?"

"Not far from here. My parents live in Nassau County about twenty minutes from here. That's where I've lived my entire life. How about you? Which house is yours?"

"Right across the way." He pointed to a high ranch with a shiny new black BMW in the driveway.

"Nice. Is that your car?"

"Yep, but don't let that change your opinion of me. I saved up for that for a few years. I'm not the stuffy rich type."

She shrugged. "I didn't think you were. I suppose you're not renting. You own that house?"

"Yep. Bought it last year. I love the neighborhood. You will, too. It's quiet, the neighbors are affable and everyone takes care of their property. There's a true sense of pride living here. Plus, the beach is twenty minutes away. That's just an added bonus."

Sipping the last of her wine, she noticed Ben was done with his as well. "So far, I'm enjoying it here, though this really is my first day."

As they both finished their wine, she got up and gently grabbed Ben's glass.

"It's been great meeting you, and I'd love to chat, but I really need to turn in. It's been a long day and my eyes are starting to close on their own."

"The pleasure's all mine, Jacqueline. Stop by anytime."

He grabbed two pieces of chocolate out of the box and popped one in his mouth.

"Just want to make sure I do my part in helping you out." With that, he winked and started to walk away. "Have a good night! Thanks for the cocktail!"

"Good-night, Ben."

Dizzy perhaps from the wine, the exhaustion, or her short meeting with Prince Charming, Jacqueline desperately needed to get some sleep.

Pleased with herself for a job well-done, she flicked the lights off, slid under the sheets, and allowed her body to float into a peaceful slumber.

Chapter 5: Framed

When Jacqueline woke up, she looked outside and noticed the sky was a gloomy shade of gray. While the weather forecast called for sunny skies later that weekend, the morning was chock-full of bleakness as droplets of rain splattered against the pane. Cracks of thunder bellowed from above, and the creaking of the tree branches made Jacqueline want to crawl back under the covers.

Her body ached from all of the work she accomplished the previous day. Tilting her neck so that she could get it to crack, she slid out of bed and stretched to try and loosen her sore muscles.

She had a flash of memory from something she had dreamt about during the night, but couldn't quite recall the details. She only knew that there had been an energetic golden retriever in it.

Dismissing it, she stood up. *Ah, a hot shower is just what I need.* Dragging her feet along the plush rug, she made her way to the shower and turned the water on full-blast, wishing she could stay in there forever.

Unfortunately, without a water heater, she had five minutes before the temperature cooled. Ice cubes flew directly out of the faucet, stabbing her skin like tiny claws.

When she got out, she put her long hair in a ponytail, applied moisturizer to her rosy cheeks, and threw on a pair of jeans and a long-sleeved T-shirt.

She was no model, but she was naturally pretty. Though she was slender, she had definite muscle tone, which was evident when she wore even the least-revealing clothes.

As she looked around her new rental, she couldn't help but feel proud. *This is all mine...for now.*

Remembering that the landlords had offered to sell it to her if she wanted it, she started calculating whether she could afford it. *Coffee first, then I'll start doing the math.*

She made enough for six cups, planning to drink at least two of them to get through the day, and then maybe freeze the rest for an iced coffee later.

Just after she poured her first, her doorbell rang. It was Benjamin, her friendly neighbor from last night.

"Hi Benjamin! I mean, Ben, Benny? Ben. Sorry!"

Laughing at her, he tried his best to give her a dirty look but couldn't quite manage. Even though her hair was still wet and pushed back in a ponytail, it was clear she looked amazing to him.

"Nice recovery. I'll let it slide this time. Just plain Ben will suffice. Let's start over, shall we? Good morning, Jacqueline."

Chuckling now, she put her hand over her mouth and opened the door all the way. "Good morning, Ben."

Seeing that he was carrying something in his hands, she glanced toward the bag and then back at Ben.

"Nothing fancy. Just bagels and cream cheese. Thought you might be hungry this morning."

"You brought me breakfast? Why, thank you! I don't know what to say. That's so kind of you, but may I ask why? I'm sorry, where are my manners? Please, come on in!"

"Thanks. To answer your question, no real reason. I figured you might be hungry and probably didn't have a chance to go grocery shopping yet since you just moved in, so I picked up some food."

As if to avoid appearing like a stalker, he explained himself a bit better.

"I'm not going to lie. I was hungry too. They're not *all* for you." He winked as he wrapped his arms around the paper bag.

"Well, I have to say, you made my morning. You must've smelled the coffee brewing, 'cause I just made a few cups. How do you take yours?"

"Just milk and sugar, thanks!"

"I admit, I'm a bit hungry. This is perfect."

"My pleasure. So, what's on your agenda today?"

"Ha, well, since you asked, today I have the pleasure of painting. It's probably not necessary, but it's my first place that I can call my own, even though I'm only renting. I want it to be special and personalized." He nodded, indicating that he was listening. "It's not exciting, I know, but I figure it's best to get the hard part done first. I'm a thrill-seeker, can't you tell?"

Something about her had obviously caught his fancy. "Need some help?"

She finished chewing on her bagel and looked surprised. "You mean painting? You'd actually help me?"

"Sure! Why not?"

"My own father didn't even offer to help me paint. It's not exactly fun, you know."

"Oh, I beg to differ with you. It can definitely be fun."

"Hey, I'm not going to argue with you. Beggars can't be choosers. If you're offering to help, then I'm accepting. But what's the catch?"

"Not a thing. Well, maybe one thing. I might get hungry later and then you'll have to let me buy you lunch a little later this afternoon."

"You're helping me and buying me lunch? Not to mention, you brought breakfast. I'll make a counteroffer. Lunch, but I'm buying."

"Ah, you fell into my trap. I get what I want—a free lunch and a beer!"

"Wait a minute. Who said anything about beer?"

"Me, just now. Didn't you hear me? Where I come from, everyone knows you have to have a beer when the job is done. I think we'll finish up by six tonight. That's the perfect time for a beer and there just happens to be a pub right down the block. Walking distance, actually. It's very convenient. That is, if your tired legs can make it."

Always up for the challenge and enjoying the flirt, she smiled. "Sure. You're on, but I'll make you eat those words later when you're the one who's too tired to walk."

"We'll see about that!" As he finished the last of his bagel and refilled his coffee, he helped put the breakfast dishes away.

Coming up behind her as she washed them, he was closer than he had been before and she felt a little uncomfortable. She was definitely attracted to him and didn't mind the closeness, but she didn't want to make any assumptions about his feelings toward her. It was obvious he enjoyed her company—otherwise he wouldn't be there—but he could also very well be just a friendly neighbor who happened to be extremely handsome.

"Silly question, but do you have an extra paintbrush, Jacqueline?"

She even liked the way he said her name. "As a matter of fact I do. And I have an extra roller! I guess you can say that I'm always prepared."

"Awesome. I'll start covering up the rugs and the furniture. Want to start in the living room?"

"Sure. Gee, thanks!" This was a dream come true. With Ben's help, they might just be finished with the living room by dinnertime. This was going to cut her time in half. He had already begun painting by the time she was done cleaning the kitchen. "So, Ben, what do you do on days when you're not helping your new neighbor paint?"

"Believe it or not, I do work—just not this week. I'm on a very-much-needed vacation."

"Oh my goodness, and you're stuck spending it by helping me?"

"It's my pleasure, truly." When she gave him a look of disbelief, he explained himself a bit more. "I work in an office, where I'm sitting at my desk every single day, editing articles for the newspaper and magazines that we distribute." Without diverting from his painting, his continued. "I love the job, but it does a number on your eyes after a while. It can be more tiring to sit on your bum staring at a computer screen then it is to do real strenuous labor. I won't complain though. It's better than my previous job as a salesperson. The money was fantastic but the hours were grueling.

"Anyhow, I'm one of the few that enjoys painting. I'm pretty good at it too, if I do say so myself."

Noticing that the edges of the walls were taped and the small corner that he had painted already looked perfect, she was embarrassed at her horrible painting skills. Smirking at him, she said, "Hmm, maybe I'll paint the middle of the wall."

Laughing now, he said, "I think that's the best idea you've had all morning, Jackie!"

Ignoring his sarcastic remark, she pressed on. "Editor, huh? That sounds like it can be quite interesting."

"Oh, it is. Especially when the article is a good one, but it can also be exhausting. Imagine trying to edit pages upon pages about statistics, or something equally as painful." He bent down to get more paint on the brush. "There are days when I question the reason I went into editing in the first place. I guess that's how it is with any job. You take the good with the bad. How about you? What do you do to occupy your time?"

The paint was already covering half of the living room wall. It looked like they were getting somewhere. Admiring their work, she smiled. "Interestingly enough, I work at an advertising agency. We're the ones that make up the little jingles that probably sell your magazines!"

"Really? Well now, that's pretty exciting!"

"Well, sort of. Like you said, some ads can be really boring. Others I get really excited about. Did you see the one about Sleek Silk body lotion?"

"Though I'm a little embarrassed to say it, I have."

"Well before you say anything negative about it, I made that one up."

"Truly?"

"Yes, and I'm quite proud of it! Thanks to that ad alone, our profits have more than doubled." She flashed a shy smile at him. Usually self-effacing by nature, she was uncomfortable with bragging, even if she clearly deserved the recognition.

"Fantastic. I love it! I didn't know you had such talent."

"Me neither. I'm just lucky I got hired there." She turned away and bit her lower lip. Frustrated with herself for opening a can of worms, she cringed.

"Lucky? Why would you say that?"

Her paint-strokes slowed as she recalled that dark time in her life. It was the only part of her past she regretted. But she wasn't a very good liar, so she decided to 'fess up.

"Well, I have a record. Can you believe that? Little innocent me with a rap sheet?"

His painting stopped altogether. "A record? You? What could you have done to end up with an arrest? Let me guess, murder?"

She rolled her eyes and shook her head. "No. Although after what I went through, I felt like I could've committed murder! It wasn't even my fault, except that I had bad judgment. I hung out with a group of delinquents who were into partying and stealing and God knows what else."

He was all ears now. "I had no idea they were even on drugs. That shows you how naïve I was. *Was*, in the past tense. Now, I'm cognizant about who I spend my time with and exercise a bit more caution."

Realizing she had only met Ben last night and was now spending the day in her new house without anyone knowing where she was or who *he* was, she realized just how naive she must seem. For all she knew, he might not even live across the street.

Ben was intrigued now. "What happened?"

"Well, we all went out one night. My friend Shelby—if you want to call her a friend—picked all of us up in a shiny, brand-new Mercedes. She claimed her parents were rich and that it was her father's car. I didn't question her one bit, but I should've known better.

"The rest of the guys in the car just laughed and treated it like garbage—smoking in it, flicking their ashes everywhere and spilling their drinks without a care in the world. They were acting like a bunch of adolescent misfits."

"I'm familiar with the type."

"Yeah, well, we went out to a club that was for teenagers. It was supposed to be only a dance club, but everyone knew the bartenders and they served alcohol to minors even though it was illegal. My friends were first in line and began drinking heavily.

"I was sixteen years old. I didn't have a license, but my father had been secretly teaching me how to drive since I was fourteen. A little bonding between the two of us that we didn't share with my mother."

"Your dad sounds like a cool guy." Ben seemed to want to keep the conversation light, as if he didn't want her to feel awkward, though she loosened up as she continued.

"He is, but I almost wish I never had those driving lessons. By the time we all decided to leave, Shelby and the gang were ossified, completely wasted. She couldn't even get the damn key in the ignition. Montgomery spent the better part of the evening tossing his cookies in the street and Chad was slurring his words so badly, there was no way either of them could speak, much less drive." Ben gave her his full attention now. "Like the hopelessly responsible idiot that I often am, I took the keys. I figured that out of the four of us, it was best that I drove since I was the only one who was sober. If Shelby had driven, I would more than likely be six feet under right now." Ben nodded. There were too many stories on the news involving drunk-driving accidents. "Once I started driving, Montgomery was screaming that he had to vomit once again, and I was worried he'd wreck Shelby's dad's car even worse. In a frenzied haste, I rushed to find a safe place where I could pull over."

"Yeah, I can't say that I blame you!"

"I was well aware that I was driving way over the speed limit, but at the time, it was better than the alternative of having Montgomery vomit all over me. Chad was mumbling something incoherent and Shelby was crying. I didn't know what the hell was wrong with them. I never saw anyone so drunk and pathetic. Between the three of them, I couldn't tell you who was worse. Each of them was the perfect poster child for drug and alcohol abuse."

"Sounds like a lovely evening. What a great group of friends."

"Yeah, tell me about it. Shelby was hiding her face and I only found out after the fact that she was covering for herself because they were all doing cocaine and a variety of other drugs." She sighed for a moment in disgust. "At first, I didn't even hear the sirens until I looked in the rearview mirror. When the cop pulled me over, I tried to explain that they were just drunk and it was Shelby's father's car, but she adamantly denied it. She had the audacity to tell the cop it was *my* car! Funny enough, when she spoke to the cop, she managed to speak eloquently with only minimal slurs. I remember how amazed I was that she could pull herself together when it benefited her."

"Yeah, that strikes me as interesting as well," said Ben.

"He ran the license plate and found out it was neither of ours. The car was stolen that afternoon by Montgomery or Shelby—I'm not even sure. A man reported it earlier that day—a very pissed-off man by the name of Mr. Griego. He was also a very rich and influential man."

"Ah, so the plot thickens."

"Unfortunately, yes. Once the cop accused us, Shelby started screaming at me about 'how dare I risk getting them in trouble by stealing a car!'"

"Are you serious?"

"I couldn't believe it myself! Not only did Shelby steal the car, but during all of the cop's questioning, she slid a good-sized bag of coke in my purse and hid it underneath my wallet so when the cop brought me into the station, there it was, in plain sight."

"Didn't you report them?"

"I would have! Believe me, but I didn't think she stole it and at the time, I had no idea she was planting drugs in my bag. I've never been betrayed by friends before this incident, so I didn't think this new crowd would be any different."

"I guess there's always a first time. Wow, Jacqueline. That's horrible."

"Of course, afterwards, I couldn't understand how I'd been so easily fooled. They all got away free and clear, aside from a minor drug charge. They each had drugs in their system, but I was the one with drugs in my possession, not them. To the cops, I looked like the dealer!"

"That's unreal!"

"Mr. Griego hired fancy lawyers and he looked at me like I was a useless punk. He wanted me in jail. I spent some time in juvenile detention, and then they let me out. I never saw my lovely friends again."

"I can't imagine that you'd want to!"

"No way. Not after what they did. So, there you have it. I'm a convict. I didn't think any businesses or employment agencies would ever hire me, so I was grateful when this one did. That's why I said I was lucky. They didn't make a big deal over my arrest."

"I still can't believe you actually got convicted."

"Yeah, me neither. My lawyer claimed that all evidence pointed to me. If I had had drugs in my system, it would've been even worse! That was my one saving grace."

"Good thing! What did your parents say?"

"What could they say? They were so angry—we all were—but they believed me. I'm still irate. No one ever came to my aid. They are just a bunch of self-indulgent drug addicts. They care about nobody except themselves." She started to feel her shoulders get tense, but didn't want to darken the mood. "Anyway, enough of that. That's my story. How about some lunch?"

She was well-aware that she switched gears, but felt herself getting increasingly upset at the memory. She wanted to turn off those feelings like a light switch.

"Sounds good. Hey, thanks for sharing. I know that wasn't easy and you really didn't have to tell me any of it. I hope they got what they deserve. Karma has a way of revealing itself to the most worthy of souls. Besides, if it means anything to you, I think you're kind of sexy for an ex-con."

He looked directly at her and she couldn't help but smile.

Okay, so maybe he is interested in me after all.

Chapter 6: Tainted Friendships

"I see that you're back at work, huh, Monty?"

"Looks that way, Carmine. I told you that there was no incriminating evidence on those tapes. I'm not a stupid guy. I know where my bread's buttered; I ain't gonna mess with that. I know we have our differences, Carmine, but I'm telling you, man, I wouldn't do it."

His street slang didn't bother Carmine too much, though it drove Donovan crazy. Luckily, Donovan was out buying more tools to replace the stolen ones. He had been glad to get away for a while and avoid any additional altercations.

Staring at Montgomery with a deadpan glare, Carmine didn't say a word for a full minute. His eyes said everything he needed to say. "You're skating on thin ice, boy. Watch it."

Montgomery returned his stare like a child obeying his father. "I will old man, don't you worry about a thing." He knew he had to try to get on Carmine's good side. "Look Carmine." He paused as Carmine studied him. "I did a little partying last night. Believe it or not, there's some extra. You can have it. No hard feelings, all right?" In Montgomery's hand was a small Ziploc baggie with a thin layer of white powder inside.

"What do you think, I'm some kind of idiot? Think I was born yesterday? I'm smart enough to know that a punk like you isn't going to just hand over the good stuff." Montgomery appeared insulted. "What's in there, Inositol? Arsenic? I do one line and keel over? Is that the general idea?" Carmine was eyeing the bag. Though he was insistent that it was bogus, he was silently hoping that it was not. "I can get my own stash anytime I want. No need for you to start playing the generous drug dealer." Still, he knew that all he needed to do was taste it to tell for sure. He was hard on his luck and hadn't had a line in over a week. Since the burglary, he hadn't made up his share of the profits, and of course they couldn't report the theft to the police.

"Suit yourself, Carmine. Do you mind if I get a little high before we start our day?"

Carmine scratched his chin considering his options. "You better not be messing with me, Montgomery. Do a line—show me that it's real." At the same time, he dipped his finger in and brought a taste of the powder to his lips to lick off. One taste and he knew it was legitimate.

Montgomery brought out a mirror and a rolled-up dollar bill. He positioned his nose over the makeshift straw and held the other nostril in, enabling him to snort up the one line of coke. Smiling, he glanced at Carmine and passed the mirror.

"Give me that shit." Carmine did the same and almost at once felt better. "You done good this time, fella. Keep up the good work." With that, he snatched the rest of the baggie and stuffed it into his pocket.

Montgomery stood there empty-handed, but realized that he had made a friend and disarmed Carmine—at least for the day.

Chapter 7: Unveiling Truths

"Pizza or sushi, Jacqueline?"

"Why sushi, of course."

"Yeah, I was thinking pizza." He flashed his remarkable smile and winked. "But for you, I'm willing to compromise and get some sushi."

"Oh, thank you. How can I ever repay you?" she retorted. She was enjoying their flirtatious banter. For the time being, neither had crossed the point of no return, and their blooming relationship was still comfortable and strictly platonic.

"I'll think of a way. Don't you worry." He bumped his shoulder into hers and nudged her off of the curb a little.

"Oops, did I do that?"

"I'm quite certain it was on purpose!" She laughed as she nudged him back.

Just before they entered the restaurant, the skies opened up and a heavy downpour began saturating the ground. A bolt of lightning flashed toward them, but was too far away to be a threat.

"Hurry, get in before you get soaked!" He gently grabbed her arm and led her inside.

"Wow, that came out of nowhere, although the sky has been gray since morning. Look at it out there. Perfect day for sleeping, isn't it, Ben? Too bad we have to finish painting."

"Nah, I think I'm going to sleep, and leave you to paint all by yourself."

"That's fine. Then I guess I am going to have to drink all of those beers alone, too."

"Whoa, beers! That changes everything!"

"Ha! I thought it would."

Once the waiter came over, they looked over the menus and placed their order.

Ben tilted his head and caught eyes with Jacqueline. "So, you're a convict, huh?"

"Oh, come on! I thought we talked about that already. Everybody has some skeletons in the closet. Mine just happen to be a little worse than some and on public record. Didn't you ever do anything stupid?"

Laughing, he shook his head. "Nope, nope, can't say that I have."

Choked for words, she smirked at him. "Well, then, I guess you really are perfect."

"Finally! It's about time somebody noticed!" He reached across the table and grabbed her hand. He wanted her to know he was only fooling around. "Nah, just kidding. I actually did do some pretty stupid things. Come to think of it, I've done a lot of things I probably should've been arrested for. I was just lucky enough to never get caught."

"Well, I would've never gotten caught either if I'd known I was doing something illegal!"

"You got a point there. That was horrible what they did to you. No one should ever be set up like that, especially by people that you considered to be your friends. I hope they get what they deserve. I fully believe in karma. What goes around, comes around...or something along those lines. I usually say that cliché backwards."

"Seriously, what've you ever done?" She paused to nibble on some edamame. "My life is like an open book, yet you walk around with this mysterious aura. I'm waiting to find out what big, dark secrets you are hiding."

"Mysterious? I'm anything but mysterious. If you met any of my friends or family, they would chew your ear off about the juvenile stuff I've done."

She raised her eyebrows. "Oh, do tell!"

"Let's see, when I was fifteen I started a fire in my school."

"Ah, a serial killer, huh?"

"What?"

"Well, you know, many serial killers wet their beds, light fires, and are known for being cruel to animals. So, you have one of the telltale signs."

"Oh, right. Yes, I'm definitely a serial killer, but I love animals and my sheets have been dry for quite some time now. My past isn't *that* dark! Do I actually look like I could hurt someone?"

"Okay, go on. What happened? Did you get into trouble?"

"Nope! Like I said, never got caught. The sprinklers put the fire out after a few minutes, the hallways were soaked and the students got to go home early."

"What made you do it?"

"I forgot to study for a test."

"A test! You risked everything for fear of failing a test?"

"Yep, straight-A student. I wasn't risking that. If I brought home a B on my report card, I would've been so angry with myself!"

"You wouldn't risk grades, but you'd risk going to jail. Wow. That doesn't sound all that logical. No offense."

"No offense taken. You're right. I regret it. I think back to what could've happened and I have nightmares. I didn't even think about it at the time, but truthfully, someone could've easily died."

"True. Good thing no one was hurt. Luck was on your side that day! Okay, what else?"

Just as he was about to comment, the waiter appeared with their entrees.

Digging in, their conversation flowed effortlessly.

"So, Ben, were you always so careful?" she asked.

"I was always good-hearted," he replied. "I don't know about careful. The most outrageous thing I ever did was lock my brother in a closet by gluing the door shut."

"Oh, goodness. All of a sudden, I feel claustrophobic. I couldn't handle that! For how long, and what in the world would possess you to do something like that?"

"Couple of hours and I think my father said those exact same words! My dad had to get him out. You can't imagine the guilt—it was inconceivable. I don't know why I did it, to be honest. He used to go into the closet to hide from monsters. I thought he was silly, so one day, I locked him in. I felt so terrible afterwards especially even in his adult years, when he had to go to counseling. That in itself was a nightmare and almost cost him his life. I still feel guilty about it!"

"Counseling, why?"

"I guess he had nightmares from it. He couldn't stand to be in the dark and had a haunting case of claustrophobia."

"I bet! Why was counseling a nightmare?"

"Oh, well, no reason, really. He just happened to have a psychotic homicidal maniac sitting alongside him in his counseling group. The lunatic almost killed him."

His voice softened as he spoke, his tone getting a bit more serious. "He was responsible for murdering a few other people in the class. My brother was one of the lucky ones to escape. Don't think that doesn't weigh on my conscience daily."

"Oh my goodness! I think I actually read about that!"

The mood was beginning to grow somber as Ben recalled the days of torture his brother had gone through.

Jacqueline sensed the tension. There was a time and a place to talk about what happened, but not now. "And you said you had a pristine past. I don't know about that!"

She threw her straw wrapper at him and made him smile just a bit.

"Aren't you glad you asked?"

"Actually, I am."

"Hmm. You know what, Jackie? I hate to say it, but…this feels like a date."

Jacqueline started to tense up. She hadn't dated in over a year—not since her last breakup, and that had been about as smooth as a cactus.

"Whoa, Jackie! I'm just kidding! Do you have something against dating?"

Mustering a smile, she shook her head. "No, no, nothing like that. I just got a little taken aback is all. Everything is fine."

"No need to escape through the bathroom window. I was just kidding." Pushing his luck just a little more, he continued. "I know where you live anyway. Go on and eat your sushi."

She loved his ability to snap back into his humorous self, as if nothing weird had transpired. He was perfect for her. She didn't want to shy away, but after her sour relationship with Terrance, she was a little hesitant. "You're not the boss of me," she couldn't help but chime in.

"Oh, and believe me, I'm thankful for that!" They both burst into laughter. They were able to discover new things about each other, and delve into their pasts without skipping a beat. It was all new, yet comfortable. Jacqueline didn't want it to end. "Anyway, what are your plans for tomorrow? Let me guess, more painting?"

"Actually, no. I think we'll finish that today and then take a break. Tomorrow, I'm just going to do some light cleaning, and I have an appointment with someone."

"Ooh, a hot date, huh?"

"Well, actually, yes, you can say that," she joked, but she really wanted to gauge his reaction. She was successful. Ben's smile faded, though he quickly tried to conceal it. She enjoyed his bout of jealousy but didn't want him to be too upset. "It is definitely a hot date. One I've been craving for quite a while. It's going to be very hot and steamy and involves my shower." When she saw his reaction, she couldn't help but put him out of his misery. "The plumber is coming over to install a water heater!"

"Oh my, I think I just met the corniest girl in the world."

More laughter followed, but she was thrilled. She had played her trump card and uncovered the information she wanted—Ben was starting to get a little crush on her. Much to her pleasant chagrin, the feeling was mutual.

Later that night, they finished painting, as they had set out to do. As promised, Jacqueline won the bet that she could walk to the pub, taunting Ben the entire way there. For added effect, she even jogged halfway there, though in truth she was hurting quite a bit. Her legs were killing her and her back felt like it was going to fragment and crumble to the ground. Ben was suffering too, but certainly couldn't give in.

Once they arrived at the bar, they collapsed in the booth and waited patiently for the waiter to take their order. Both were more than anxious to get their hands on a delicious, ice-cold beer. Before they knew it, it was ten-thirty.

"Ready to call it a night, Ben?"

"We better. We have that long walk ahead of us."

"Oh, it's not even a mile. I thought you could handle it no problem!"

"Well, that was before I helped a certain someone paint, and before that same person ordered me four beers. Suffice it to say, I'm finished!"

"Well, yeah. Me too," she admitted.

They both laughed at their inability to admit defeat and walked back to their respective houses. Once he was at his door and she at hers, Ben yelled out to her. "Hey Jacqueline?"

"Shhh! You'll wake the neighborhood!"

Slurring his words just a bit, he asked "Are you free tomorrow night?"

Feeling uninhibited and without reserve, she said "Sure. For what?"

"How about dinner and a movie? I'll pick you up at six. You live so far away and all."

"Sounds good."

"And Jacqueline?"

"Yeah, Ben?" She was laughing now.

"That *will* be a date."

With those parting words, he left her speechless on her front porch as he walked into his own house, shutting his door slowly behind him.

All she could do was shake her head and laugh, a jittery sensation in her belly. *A date. Huh. I guess I walked right into that one!* She was elated as her head hit the pillow.

***

When she woke up, she couldn't understand why she felt so at peace, but then remembered her dream and smiled.

She was sitting on the front porch in a gliding swing—only in her dream, she owned the house. At her feet was a young, happy-go-lucky golden retriever. His mane was a beautiful blend of gold and blond silky hair. His milky brown eyes were wide and alert, watching over the neighborhood, wagging his tail as he noticed people passing by. Every so often, he'd swing his head backward to look at Jacqueline and flash his golden smile as she reached down to scratch him behind his ears.

She had no idea if the dog belonged to her, or even what his name was. All she knew was that while she was with him, she felt safe, calm, and secure. She also felt a genuine happiness that only occurred when he was around.

Since her parents had both worked during the day when she was growing up, they had never adopted a puppy for Jacqueline. She never had the desire to own a dog and had no actual love for them, but something about this dream made her consider rescuing one in the future.

As she began to get ready for her day, she vaguely remembered Ben shouting across the street that tonight would be an actual date, and hoped she didn't dream that too. Then she couldn't help but wonder if it was wise to date her new neighbor.

What if it didn't work out? What if it did?

Those, and a thousand more questions like them, filled her thoughts.

It's dinner and a movie. How much damage can be done?

Pulling herself together, she got dressed. The plumber was coming today and soon she would have hot water whenever she wanted, rather than having to jump in and out of the shower within five minutes. No longer would she have to endure the arctic burst of ice water rushing out from the showerhead. Needless to say, she was excited. It was the little things in life that sometimes gave her the most pleasure.

Chapter 8: Unleashed Rage

Carmine had driven to the shop a bit earlier than usual and opened it up before Donovan arrived. Always known for having a way with words, he summed up the scene with four short ones: *Son of a bitch!*

Products were knocked over, leaving a giant mess in the middle of the store, and more tools had been stolen. He ran to the secret room, tripping over a stool as he did so, and breathed a small sigh of relief that none of the safes had yet been discovered. But he theorized that it was only a matter of time.

To his astonishment, no money had been taken, but then he remembered that Donovan had vowed to leave only a few dollars in the cash register after the last burglary. They had learned an expensive lesson about the importance of dropping off excess cash at the bank.

Speaking to no one but the four walls, Carmine shook his fists and growled, "I'm gonna find out who you are and make you regret the day you were born!"

Since the last burglary, Donovan had installed outside surveillance cameras as an additional security measure. Only Carmine and Donovan were aware of them and this time, they were clever enough not to tell Montgomery. As Carmine sat down to begin watching the tapes, Donovan walked in. "What happened here?"

"What the hell do you think happened? Our night prowler was at it again. I'm getting ready to watch the tapes now. Do you want me to pause it while you go make some popcorn?"

Donovan ignored this. He was growing weary of his partner's constant negativity. "Give me a sec. Let me put this stuff down." He unloaded his mini-safe and other belongings, and then sat down next to Carmine. "Hang on one more minute. Let me lock the front door. As of this moment, we're not open for another hour."

They sat down together, hunched over the front desk as they began to watch the video. The tension in the air was as thick as mud and the anger radiated off both of them in red-hot waves. But even once they made it through most of the tape, there was still no evidence of who the burglar was.

"Dammit! Nothing."

"Hang on there, Carmine. There's still a few minutes left on the tape. Everyone slips up. This guy will, too."

"Bullshit. It's practically over. We can't get a picture of his face."

The slide bar on the bottom of the tape read 3:22:00. They had only a few minutes left to watch, but that proved to be enough.

This time, there were two thieves, and one of them got sprayed with a cleaner right through his black acrylic ski mask. While he was in the shop, he rubbed his eyes through the mask, but the stinging sensation must've been too painful to handle. As soon as the thieves walked outside, he threw the stolen goods to his partner and ripped his mask off.

Underneath was a face they recognized all too well. Without saying a word, they backed up, as if that would entitle them to a better view.

Donovan spoke first, still cool as a cucumber. "Well, I'll be dammed. It was him all along. He bulked himself up with extra clothes. He had us fooled—the little shit."

Carmine pounced up from his seat, pacing back and forth, and breathing heavily through his flared nostrils like a tormented bull. "Correction, he had *you* fooled. Not me, *you!*" Donovan watched stoically as Carmine pointed the finger at him and swept his hand across the desk, sending Post-It notes and pens onto the floor. His eyes were fixed and the color of charcoal. "I told you it was that piece of shit. Didn't I tell you? He walked in here all full of himself yesterday—thought he was king shit. That bastard looked me right in the eye and lied to my face like it was the most normal thing in the world. He looked at me like I was crazy. He wants to see crazy? I'll show him a thing or two."

"All right, Carmine. You were right. You also partied with him yesterday, so get off of your high horse already. We got our man. Now we wait."

"Bullshit. You wait. I'm going to wring his neck when he gets here." Expecting an argument from Donovan, who was usually the logical one, he received nothing but a deeply pensive look.

The darkness in his eyes showed that he just might share Carmine's anger after all. "Okay, Carmine, but we need to be smart about this." Confused by his partner's new perspective, Carmine decided to listen just this once. "Carmine, Montgomery has no clue about the outside video camera, does he?"

"Nope, not unless you told him."

"My lips were sealed. That's good. There's no chance that he'll realize what we know. Go about your business as usual. Pretend to be pissed off."

"I am pissed off."

"What else is new? You're always pissed off. What I am saying is, this time, pretend to be even more pissed off, like you don't know who did this. Play the role; don't let on that you know it was him. I want him to be caught off-guard."

"Let me get this straight. You're asking me to pretend that I think he's innocent? Have you completely gone mad?" But he sensed something different in his partner's tone, so he acquiesced. "Okay, fine. Until when?"

"We have two big jobs today in the field. The first one, you're not going to need his help on; however, the second one is a new renter who wants to install a water heater. Use the time afterwards wisely."

The mood was grave, but Carmine knew what Donovan was implying. Though they had grown accustomed to roughing people up every now and then, they had only had to do something this drastic once before, when they were robbed at gunpoint outside of a dive bar. The robber had been after their stash, which was worth well over five thousand dollars. He almost got away with it, until Carmine pulled out a knife. To date, no one had found the thief's body.

"One question," asked Carmine. "Who is the second person in the surveillance video?"

"It doesn't matter. They won't be back. I have a gut feeling they only accompanied Montgomery because Montgomery knew the layout here, sans the safes in the back room. After tonight, we won't have to worry about that. No cops have been involved. No one's the wiser. We're free and clear. You got that?"

Almost submissive, Carmine answered, "Yep." He looked away as if he were planning his future. "Sure do, and I'm looking forward to it."

"Good, don't get caught. Go about your business. Get rid of the evidence. Go home afterwards. I'll see you tomorrow first thing."

"Got it."

"Carmine?"

"Yeah, Don?"

"When the dust settles, we'll get our shit back. Until then, just take care of the perpetrator. The loss we endured is peanuts in comparison to what he's got coming to him. Make sure he doesn't step foot in here—or anywhere—again."

Chapter 9: Battle of Wits

Donovan and Carmine waited for Montgomery to arrive, each pacing the floor like a frazzled tiger.

"Unlock the door, Carmine. He'll be here any moment."

"I'm on it already."

Mixed emotions jumbled Carmine's thinking, mostly excitement, nervousness, and relentless apprehension. He looked forward to removing their main source of trouble, but he hadn't done this in a while and there was no room for error.

Like clockwork, Montgomery was always seven to fifteen minutes late. Today was no different. By ten minutes after nine, he strolled through the door, chipper as a canary, though without the pleasant whistle accompanying him.

"Morning, guys!" He removed his sweatshirt and flung it haphazardly onto the coat rack.

Donovan and Carmine exchanged glances. Donovan sensed Carmine's anger like a dog smelled a bone, and his own eyes advised him to follow their plan. Any deviation would throw them off track and give Montgomery the upper hand. There was no way Montgomery could be allowed to have the edge.

Sensing their tension, Montgomery spoke up. "What's wrong? Someone die?"

"Interesting choice of words. No, no one died, Montgomery. We were just burglarized. Again." Trying to disguise his anger and hatred for the punk standing before them, Carmine bit his lip.

Montgomery pressed on. "Oh, man. Did they get anything of value?"

"Of course they did! What did you think they took, the freaking gumball machine?" Though Donovan was typically the calm one, he was the one to lose his cool.

"Easy, okay? Relax Donovan! I was just asking!"

Now Carmine was the one silently warning Donovan to stay calm.

"First off, I'm relaxed," said Donovan. "Secondly, don't ever tell me to relax. I'm your boss. Remember that."

"Yes, sir. Sorry."

"Get your uniform on. We have a couple of jobs to do."

As he walked into the back to retrieve his uniform, Donovan motioned toward Montgomery's sweatshirt and mouthed to Carmine to make sure Montgomery took it with him. They didn't want any evidence of his arrival or his untimely dismissal.

Donovan quietly stole the keys to Montgomery's car. He planned to drive it to the bar at lunchtime. It was a normal hangout for Montgomery and no one would find it out of the ordinary to see his car there so early in the day.

"Ready to go?"

"Ready as I'll ever be!"

"Here." Carmine took the sweatshirt off the rack and threw it at Montgomery. "Supposed to be a cold one today. You might need this."

Donovan's eyes shifted from one man to the other, trying to read if anything had been revealed. Montgomery didn't appear any the wiser. Carmine seemed restrained. As far as he was concerned, all was going according to plan.

As Carmine and Montgomery piled into the work van, Montgomery looked up at the building and squinted as he saw two small black boxes on opposite sides of the doorway.

As he focused and got a better look, he recognized what they were: security cameras. He had been working there for three years and knew the building inside and out. He realized they were only recently installed.

Carmine was busy looking behind him as he backed up the van. Like the sudden shock of a Taser, Monty's memory was electrified as he thought about the cleaner that had gotten in his eyes, and how he had removed his mask once they were outside. Shackles of bewilderment wrapped tightly around his body like a cumbersome cloak. They knew. That means they saw his partner in crime, his girlfriend Shelby. He surmised that they would try to get to her as well.

His next emotion was that of full-blown anger, the kind that doesn't have to get heated in order to boil, but starts off as a whistling kettle. He peered at Carmine and wanted to kill him right then and there. They were playing him like a fiddle, except now, he owned the bow.

Chapter 10: Monty's Revenge

Montgomery quietly reached down into his tool belt to make sure he had his scissors on him. They would have to suffice. The only other sharp tools were still in the toolbox.

His hands trembled as indignation streamed through his pumped-up veins. His emotions varied from vehemence to anticipation of things to come. Donovan and Carmine had tricks up their sleeves. And he had a strong feeling that those tricks would be deadly. "So Carmine, you didn't even see the guy's face, huh?"

"Nope. We'll get him, though. Don't you worry, Montgomery."

Infuriated still, it was getting more difficult to fake it. "What jobs do we have today?" He noticed a knife on Carmine's tool belt. Not that a knife is all that uncommon, but then he glanced downward toward Carmine's ankle. It was well-concealed, but definitely there. Carmine had his gun with him.

"Look at the clipboards." Carmine motioned to the floor behind the driver's seat with his free hand. "It's all there."

Montgomery calculated whether he would be capable of finishing the jobs by himself, and decided that he could.

It was illegal to carry a gun on the job, and anyway there would be no need for it. They were traveling to a decent and safe neighborhood. There would only be one reason and one reason only to carry a gun. Carmine was planning to kill him.

Think fast, Montgomery.

They were approaching a park on their right-hand side. It was still closed for the winter, though there were only a few more days until it reopened for spring.

"Oh man. Carmine, pull over."

"What?"

"Pull over. Quick! I'm going to be sick. I drank too much last night and this morning's breakfast is starting to disagree with me. I'm going to barf up my cookies, man, hurry!"

He doubled over in a theatrical demonstration of excruciating agony. He had enough experience to play the role flawlessly.

Carmine pulled the van over to the side of the road.

"Pull in the park, Carmine. I got some shit on me. If a cop comes over to see what we're up to, we'll both get arrested."

"You brought drugs to a client's house? What the hell is wrong with you?" Carmine pulled way into the park behind some trees, looking behind him to make sure they weren't followed. If a cop pulled them over, they wouldn't only get arrested for cocaine, but for Carmine's gun as well. He couldn't risk it. There was no way he was going to allow Montgomery to put as much as a wrinkle in his devious plan. "I can't believe you, Monty. How much freaking cocaine do you have on you?"

"A lot, man. I have a buyer after work." Montgomery stepped out of the van and staggered over to a bush, acting as if he was vomiting. "Oh man, this morning's eggs. *Ugh.*"

"I don't want a detailed description, just finish up and let's get the hell out of here!" Carmine got out of the van and positioned himself by a tree to relieve himself. He started whistling as he did so—a habit that he never shed—and Montgomery took that as his cue. With steadfast speed, Montgomery raced up behind him. Carmine's fly was still open, and Montgomery had the element of surprise working for him.

With one hand, he wrapped his arm around Carmine's neck and with the other, he jabbed both blades of the scissors into Carmine's throat. His body fell backward and his head hit the ground, his eyes pleading as he grasped at the handle and tried to push Montgomery away. As he struggled, Montgomery reached for Carmine's gun but knew that if he shot, someone would hear the blast. Instead, he reached for Carmine's knife as Carmine struggled, still gurgling and fighting for his life. "You found out it was me, didn't ya? Thought you were going to kill me today, huh? I saw the cameras just as we were leaving the parking lot. You should've pulled out of the parking lot sooner. I also saw your gun. Nice touch." Standing above him, he watched as Carmine fought to stay alive, but he was losing way too much blood. "Sayonara, my friend."

The jagged edge of his own knife was thrust directly into Carmine's chest. Montgomery wasn't sure if he had struck his heart or not, as Carmine's body jerked rapidly for a moment before he succumbed to death.

Unlike Carmine, who had only killed once before, Montgomery had previous experience with it and never got caught. He was confident this murder wouldn't be any different. As he looked around nervously, he didn't see anyone approaching. The radio from the van was still on, a newscaster softly announcing the midmorning traffic.

Montgomery initially considered hiding the body under a pile of leaves, but since the park would be open in a few days, he determined a different approach.

As expected, Carmine was dead weight. Montgomery grabbed him from behind, dragging his lifeless body toward the van.

Frantic to beat the clock without getting caught, he looked around for something to wrap the body in.

Fortunately, the odds worked in his favor as there were plenty of tools and supplies in the back of the van. He located a large tarp typically used for transporting items that might contain leaky substances. It was perfect. He used it to securely wrap Carmine's body, sealing it tightly with the extra ropes used to secure equipment.

Before lugging into the van the body, he made certain that blood would not drain.

He kicked a massive pile of dead leaves over the pool of blood that dripped onto the ground, hoping a hungry animal would lick it up or a heavy rainstorm would ensue before anyone noticed.

His hands were also full of blood, but there was plenty of cleaner and water in the van. He washed up the best that he could and then took off his blood-stained shirt and pants, threw them in the back of the van, retrieving clean ones from the box of extras.

Satisfied, he climbed in the driver's seat and whistled the remainder of the song that Carmine had been whistling when the scissors were jammed into this flesh, ending the catchy tune, as well as his life.

Chapter 11: Recognition of the Past

Though he had a couple of ideas traveling through his mind, he wasn't quite sure which was the most foolproof. Storing them all in a pocket of his memory, Montgomery made it to his first appointment on time. He didn't want to be late, since that would only cause the customer to call the shop and rat him out. Any alarms sounding in Donovan's direction would only mean devastation.

No, he had to play this just right. Normally, he would have had more time to deliberate. His previous kills had been pre-meditated, but this one was right off the cuff.

He knew of an ideal dumping spot for the body behind the dunes of the shoreline but had to figure out a way to get there without being spotted. He decided he would go there after dark, taking the back roads.

Whistling in an attempt to appear relaxed, he pulled into the driveway of his first customer. The truth was that he couldn't get that awful tune out of his head.

As he strolled up the driveway, the homeowner greeted him at the door.

"Good morning, Mr. Welsh," he said. "How are you doing today?"

"Very well, thank you."

"I understand that you are having some trouble with your sink getting clogged?"

Mr. Welsh didn't seem to have any clairvoyant visions about the homicide that had taken place only moments prior, or that there was a dead body going through the beginning stages of rigor mortis in the van. Everything was as it should be. Montgomery's nerves finally calmed.

"Yeah, started about two days ago. It keeps filling up and takes forever to drain. I used the snake that I have, but this time, it's not working. I have a few other issues I'll need you to look at, too."

"Not to worry, I'll have them fixed in no time."

In his head, he kept reciting the same words over and over. *Don't draw attention to yourself; don't be too nice, don't be mean. The client cannot call the office again. Just get the job done and get it done right.*

Instead of just fixing the issue, he replaced some old parts with sparkling new ones, without notifying the customer. By the time he was done, the sink was as good as new.

"All done, Mr. Welsh."

"Thank you. Anything I should do to keep it working?"

"Nope! There was just some blockage, but it is draining as it should. You have yourself a good day."

"Here, for you." The customer handed him a ten-dollar bill.

"Oh, thank you, but that's okay. No tip is necessary."

"Well, all right! Have a good day yourself."

The paperwork for the next jobs was for a Ms. Florens. He drove up to her house and struggled to move the water heater up to her garage. Typically, two men were needed for such a job. He walked to her front door and rang the bell.

"Ms. Florens?"

Her eyes stung at the sight of him. She was thankful she was already leaning on the wall, otherwise she might've stumbled. Could her luck be so awful that the one plumber she had dialed happened to employ him, of all people?

She answered curtly, wanting nothing more than to slam the door on him. "Yes."

"I'm here to install a water heater."

To add insult to injury, he didn't recognize her. After all he had put her through, he had the audacity to forget? Was he that burned out? "Sure, right this way."

Her first instinct was to refuse to let him in, and summon up an excuse that she'd changed her mind or had hired another plumber. But it wasn't as if he recognized her anyway. And if she didn't let him in, she might have to wait another week to hire a different plumber.

She led him to the garage, and he got to work. She sat and in her living room, fumbling with the remote control and wishing he'd hurry up.

The more she allowed herself to recollect her time at the detention center, the more she wanted to give him a piece of her mind. Montgomery.

The same Montgomery who had vomited while she had unknowingly driven them around town in a stolen car. The same Montgomery who had partied with Shelby and didn't lift a finger to help her when the cops slapped handcuffs on her wrists and placed her under arrest.

It was just her luck. The same person responsible for stealing her freedom was installing her water heater. She only hoped he knew what he was doing.

After an hour, he called out to her.

"Ms. Florens?"

"Yes?" She rolled her eyes.

"Can you please turn on the hot water in all of the rooms and make sure you have some warmth coming out of there?"

"Yes, one minute."

He must have done the job right. The water was steaming hot in all the sinks.

"It's all good!" she called back to him. She wanted to add, "except for the part where you took away six months of my life," but refrained.

Within a minute, he was back at her door with the paperwork. Hesitating, she invited him in.

"Just need ya to sign there and there and initial here. Let me just show you the controls and you're all set."

He wrote his signature, too, and handed her a copy for her records. He then took off his glasses and placed them on the edge of the couch.

"Let's walk in the garage so I can show you how to work it. You don't need to do much, but just in case it ever stops working, there's a switch for you to push, here and here. This bulky manual is for you. Everything that you need to know is in there."

"Okay, I think I got it."

"Great, do you have any questions?"

"Nope. All good."

She stared intently at him now, looking for a reaction, an apology, or recognition—but got nothing in return.

"Have a good day!" he called out to her, but she couldn't manage to say anything back. Everything that came to the tip of her tongue was vile and offensive, so she thought it best to keep quiet.

As she walked back into her house, she saw his glasses on the couch. A speck of blood was on the tip of the lens.

Oh, shoot. I hope I can catch him and that he didn't hurt himself. Eh, who am I kidding, who cares if he hurt himself?

"Hey! Hey!" She ran to the van in time to catch up to him. "You forgot these." She was a tad winded. He was putting his tools in the side door when she saw it. "Oh my goodness, are you all right?"

A blanket partially covered with blood lay in plain sight, though she could only see the corner of it. The body was well-hidden, thanks to Montgomery's planning, but the tarp must not have been sealed as tight as he had thought. "Yes, I'm fine. I just hurt myself earlier." He was getting paranoid, aching to do a line. He wanted her to go back into the house.

Not seeing an ounce of blood on him, she couldn't help but ask. "Where?"

"What?"

"Where did you cut yourself? That looks like a lot of blood. I'll go get my first aid kit."

That was it. He snapped.

"Look, I'm fine, okay? I already bandaged myself up when it happened." The edginess in his voice and emptiness in his eyes caught her full attention.

"Okay fine. I just thought you were hurt."

The wheels were now spinning. That was way too much blood for a simple cut. Before she could think anything of it, he interrupted her thoughts.

"I know you."

"What?"

"You're Jacqueline."

"Yes."

"Jacqueline Florens."

"Yes."

"And you know me."

She gave in, defeated. "Yes."

"Have a nice day, Jacqueline."

Her heart was now in her throat. She didn't quite know why she was scared, but she was.

Chapter 12: Destiny or Karma

Feeling as if she'd just stepped through a minefield, she wanted nothing more than to wipe the feeling of dread from her mind. Seeing Montgomery again after all these years made her feel vulnerable, and the episode near his van had sent bad vibes circling through her mind like a twisting kaleidoscope.

Acknowledging the possibility that she was looking too much into things, she decided it was best to let it go. Whatever Montgomery was up to was none of her business. After what he and Shelby had put her through, she didn't care if his wound caused him to bleed to death, as long as she didn't have to clean up the mess. Since she never had to see him again, it didn't concern her.

Once she had finished cleaning up and organizing everything to her liking, she deemed her house livable and granted herself permission to take the rest of the afternoon for herself. She curled up on her bed, clicked on the television and let an old-time, black-and-white movie lure her into a different world. Before she knew it, she had fallen asleep. She was surprised when she woke up and looked at the clock.

Four o'clock! I must've really been tired. I'd better get myself in gear.

She recalled Ben saying he would pick her up at six—not that he really had to go too far. Relieved that she still had plenty of time to get ready, she made herself a fresh pot of coffee and sat by the kitchen window, admiring the flowers preparing to bloom.

Now that she had the water heater, she looked forward to taking a shower that, for the first time since moving into her new home, she would actually enjoy. The stress of the day melted away as the hot water soothed her aching muscles, trickling onto her shoulders and down her back. She took advantage of the consistent flow of warmth, and spent twenty minutes enjoying it without one negative thought stabbing her mind.

As expected, Ben arrived at the door at six o'clock sharp. He had a small bouquet in his hands and had actually washed his car for the occasion. Jacqueline hurried to put the flowers in a vase, checked the windows and doors to ensure they were locked, and then she and Ben were on their way.

It was safe to say if each date had a report card, this one would pass with flying colors. It was ten-thirty by the time they arrived back home and although she wanted to invite him in, Jacqueline stuck to her guns, ending the evening with a light kiss on the doorstep.

"Thank you so much. That was a lot of fun…for a date," she winked.

"My pleasure. Hey, if you're not doing anything this weekend, feel free to stop by."

"I just might do that!"

He waved as he got to his front step and they both closed their doors behind them.

Oh no! Ugh. I completely forgot. Jacqueline, what is wrong with you, scatterbrain?

Toilet paper. The one thing you cannot go without regardless of who you are.

She grabbed her keys and her purse before venturing out into the dark night to visit the twenty-four-hour drug store. One of the highlights of her community was that there was one within two miles of her home. It only took her five minutes to get there and she was happy that within ten minutes, she'd be back home, enjoying the comfort of her own bed.

As she drove back home, she recalled the evening's date and was thankful that her life was once again on track in the direction she had so meticulously mapped out.

She hadn't been driving for longer than a minute when out of nowhere, she spotted a figure lying in the middle of the road—directly in front of the wheels of her car. Jacqueline tried to apply full pressure on the brakes and swerve to the right, but it was too late; there was nothing in the world she could do.

The horrific sound of the impact was so intense, it echoed in her mind hours later; she knew it was not just a shredded tire or a piece of garbage. Something had popped. She had felt it, and it was too large to be a cat. She cringed as she realized it might've been a large dog.

Tears were already rolling down her cheeks as she pulled over and exited the vehicle. Though it was a dark night, the illumination from the lamppost guided her and enabled her to get a better view. As she got closer, her eyes widened and her legs felt weak. "No! Help! Someone help!" She ran back into the car to grab her cell phone and dial 911. "Hello, please come quick! There's been a terrible accident." She ran out of the car to wave down any traffic heading in her direction. "I was driving and just hit a pedestrian; she's not moving!"

She tried to help the girl on the ground, but knew enough not to move her. No other cars were on the road, but Jacqueline set out the two flares that she had, just in case. She was lightheaded and felt as though she would pass out at any moment but knew she had to stay calm. The person she had just hit needed help more than she did. She had to do everything in her power to save her. Even though only a minute had passed, it felt like a lifetime.

She dialed 911 again. "Hello, please. I just called. Please send someone quick. There's a lot of blood. I don't think she's doing too well. Please hurry."

"The paramedics are on their way, ma'am. Please calm down. They will be there soon. Do not move the body; you can do more harm than good. Someone will be there shortly."

"Okay, thank you." Jacqueline couldn't stand on her own two feet any longer. She staggered to the girl and kneeled down in front, trying not to look but finding it difficult to turn away.

Within minutes, the police and paramedics were on the scene, lifting the lifeless girl onto a stretcher. Jacqueline walked over as they were lifting her into the ambulance and offered her assistance. That's when she finally got a good look.

There was no way the girl was alive. Her head had nearly separated from her body.

As the paramedics lifted the girl further into the light, Jacqueline couldn't believe her eyes. It was too much to bear. She recognized the girl on the stretcher and that girl was now dead.

Jacqueline's own body gave out and she collapsed to the ground.

Chapter 13: Transformation

Jacqueline woke up in the hospital with her parents sitting on the edge of her bed. A policeman slowly paced the floor.

Disoriented, she attempted to speak. "What happened? Why am I here?"

"Jackie, you're okay, honey," her mother told her. "You just fell and bumped your head. It's just a minor bruise, but you were unconscious for a short while. Your father and I were worried sick and we raced here as fast as we could."

Underneath the blankets, Jacqueline wiggled her fingers and toes to assure herself that she wasn't paralyzed. Everything was a blur—she couldn't remember why she was there. Within minutes, however, it was clear.

"How do you feel?" Her father had always been a little calmer than her overbearing mother.

"I feel a little out of it, but I'm not hurt. At least I don't think I am."

Her parents both just nodded, and Jacqueline looked up. She caught eyes with the policeman, who walked over to the bed. "Jacqueline, I'm Detective Brown. Do you remember anything about the accident that happened earlier this evening?"

In an instant, the fuzzy layer of sleep peeled away and she did remember. A throbbing pain shot up toward her neck and straight to her head. Her migraine was now back with a vengeance and once again, she started to feel dizzy. The entire room swayed like a flimsy hammock hanging from a frail tree. "I do. How is she?"

She wanted to confirm the girl's identity, but was still too scared to ask. She had hoped that what she remembered wasn't really the truth, but just an awful dream she couldn't shake.

The detective shook his head. "Unfortunately, she didn't make it. I just need to ask you some questions and then once the doctors give their okay, you can go."

Detective Brown seemed to lack any kind of emotion or compassion. In fact, Jacqueline's first impression was that he was downright cold-hearted. He was a big guy, close to six-foot- five and three hundred pounds. He had a deep, intimidating voice and dark brown eyes—the kind whose stare could turn water into ice cubes.

"Okay, sure, I'd be happy to help in any way that I can. I'll tell you everything that happened."

Ignoring her, he started plugging away. "First, where were you going?"

"I was coming home from the drugstore. I...I had to get toilet paper. I know it's silly, but I had none in the house. I had forgotten all about it. Since I had just recently moved into the house, I'd been working nonstop on getting it clean and organized. I had a date and when I got home, I looked in the pantry..."

He pressed on. "What time did you leave your house?"

"Like I said, I had a date and must have gotten home around ten-thirty or so."

"Ms. Florens, what time did you *leave* to get your necessities?"

"I guess around ten-forty."

She stiffened up and tried to calm down. Her nerves had gotten the better of her.

"Okay, so, tell me exactly what happened. I would appreciate it if you were honest and didn't leave anything out."

"Well, I was driving home..."

"Were you drinking?"

His interruptions were wearing thin. He wasn't just asking questions. He was being downright rude.

"No."

"Drugs?"

"No!"

Her father interjected. "Listen, my daughter isn't on trial. I can tell you for sure that she doesn't do drugs, nor has she ever done drugs. She said she would help you in any way possible. It would be kind of you to show her the same respect."

"Mm-hm. Sir, would you and your wife mind waiting outside?"

"It was an accident! My daughter is not on trial!"

"Maybe not yet, but if necessary, I can make sure that she will be. Now, please go wait outside."

"Dad, Mom, it's okay. I don't mind. I'll answer any of Detective Brown's questions. I'll be fine."

With obvious concern, her parents hesitated before opening the door to the hallway and leaving the room.

"Okay, so you weren't drinking and you weren't doing drugs," continued the detective. "What was it? Were you tired? Were the street lamps not working? Were the roads wet? Explain the situation as you remember it."

"What? No. The roads were fine."

Shaking his head, the detective wrote down some notes. The silence became unbearable. "So, tell me, Ms. Florens, how did it happen?"

Though he had said it was standard questioning, Jacqueline felt it was much more than that. She had butterflies in the pit of her stomach, but she wasn't sure if it was because she was nervous or livid. Did he really think she did this on purpose?

"Detective Brown, it was dark out."

"Uh-huh. It sure was."

"I was driving the speed limit…"

"That's good. I guess you learned your lesson last time you were speeding."

That confirmed it. The person who had been lying smack-dab in the middle of the street had indeed been who she thought it was: Shelby Winfred.

The same girl who only a few years earlier had framed Jacqueline for crimes she would've never committed.

And Detective Brown knew; he knew Shelby and was well aware of the connection between the two of them, which was why he was implying that she had done this on purpose. He was trying to find loopholes in her story—except there weren't any. She was being honest. Though she was beginning to feel nauseous, she continued on anyway. "Before I knew it, I saw a figure in front of my car. I slammed on the brakes, but it didn't help. It was too late. I…" She had to pause to get her breath, and the reality of what happened finally sunk in. Her voice dwindled to a whisper. "I felt the impact underneath my car." She had to swallow to keep from vomiting. The thought of killing anyone, even someone as detestable as Shelby, was unbearable. "If I had to venture a guess, I'd say she passed out in the middle of the road, or maybe tripped. I can't think of any other reason for her being in the middle of nowhere that late at night."

"And that's it?"

"Then I called nine-one-one. I set out some flares and tried to talk to the girl, you know, to try and soothe her, but

Detective, I believe she was already unconscious or dead. My attempts were futile, but I didn't want to give up hope."

"That's interesting, Jacqueline. Are you aware of whom that girl was?" She nodded and looked down, tears pooling in her eyes. "So you realize that you killed Shelby Winfred. I believe the two of you had a rocky past."

Whereas before, she had averted eye contact, his last sentence forced her to meet his stabbing gaze dead-on. Exasperation was pressurizing inside her like a geyser getting ready to discharge. "With all due respect, if you are suggesting that I killed her on purpose, think again. I wasn't aiming for her. It wasn't like I came back from a wonderful date, looked at a tracking device for Shelby, and headed out on a mission to run her over. Look in my car. You'll see I went out for toilet paper. If you'll check my house, you'll see there is no toilet paper! That's the only reason I went out. It wasn't to kill a girl I haven't seen in years." She wiped the sweat from her brow. She didn't care about respect for a detective, or even getting arrested. The idea that she could kill anyone on purpose was ludicrous and she was infuriated at Detective Brown for even thinking it.

"Thanks for clearing that up, Jacqueline, but I didn't accuse you of anything."

"You didn't have to. You're standing in front of me stone- faced, doing your best to get a reaction from me. Well, congratulations. You got one. I was a naïve teenager when all that bullshit went down with Shelby and her crew. I was angry. Wouldn't you have been? Hell, I will admit it. I am *still* angry at what I had to go through, but anger never justifies murder. If I was going to kill her, don't you think I would have done so years ago? Do you really think I would've waited all of this time? Just when things in my life are starting to get back to normal, do you seriously believe I would be *that* stupid?"

"Thank you for your time. You've been most helpful. Take care of that bump on your head."

That was it. The detective turned on his heel and walked out, and Jacqueline was mad as hell. She wanted to jump out of bed and chase him down the hall. He had pushed buttons she didn't even know she had. Her temper didn't expose itself often, but some people have a fury that builds, creating a volcano when a lone spark hits the flame. Hers had just erupted.

Chapter 14: Recovery

The head nurse hadn't wanted to release her, but Jacqueline had insisted and signed herself out at three in the morning. She didn't want to stay there for a minute longer than necessary. As she walked out the automatic doors with her parents, she shuddered as she watched no one other than Montgomery walk in. His lingering gaze penetrated through her skin, causing an onset of chills. Their recent chance meetings were disturbing.

She assumed that he'd heard what happened to Shelby, although she didn't realize they had still been that close. Would Shelby have listed him as someone to contact should anything happen to her?

Either way, she couldn't wait to get out of the hospital. Jacqueline's parents didn't drop her off at home until four in the morning. Her car had been impounded by the police for evidence, to be returned upon inspection. She didn't even know if she wanted it back after what had happened. She'd be just as content to leave the car with them and buy a new one.

Knowing that her nerves were rattled, Jacqueline fell asleep with a little help from a friend—a sleeping pill the doctors had prescribed to her to help ease her stress and anxiety.

The next day was a Saturday and she slept well past noon. She probably could've slept a little later if the incessant pounding on the door didn't jolt her from her pleasant dream.

Paranoid that it might be Detective Brown coming to arrest her after all, she rose, put on her robe, and quickly brushed her teeth. She threw her hair in a ponytail and abruptly answered the door, expecting an altercation.

"Oh, Ben! Hi!" Initially, she was a little perturbed that he had woken her, but she was very relieved to see him standing in front of her instead of the detective.

"Whoa! Sleeping a little late, are you? I thought I had you home at a respectable hour."

"Oh, you did." She let out a deep breath. "Ben, I might as well tell you now. Something horrible happened last night." The lines on her face expressed obvious anxiety.

"Jacqueline, are you okay? What happened? It must be serious."

"Yeah, it is. It was a terrible evening. I'm fine, physically, I guess. It's the mental part that continues to be a problem." She led them over to the kitchen. "Come, sit down. Do you want some coffee? I need to shake off this weary feeling."

"Sure, sounds good. Please don't leave me hanging. What's going on?"

He sat down at the kitchen table, fumbling with the napkin dispenser, while Jacqueline brewed some ground roast. Still trying to collect her thoughts and make sense of what happened, she took a minute before speaking. "Well, last night after we got home, I realized I was completely out of toilet paper. I know, sounds ridiculous, right? I had no choice, so I went to the drugstore to pick up a few rolls."

"Jackie, you could've taken a roll from my house. I'm quite certain I could have spared it!"

"Well, it's a two-minute drive. I figured I'd be there and back within ten minutes. I always run out for last-minute items, never thinking there'd be a price to pay...until last night."

"All right, so what happened?"

"On the way back, I was driving the normal route and before I could do anything about it, I noticed something directly in front of my car. I slammed on my brakes, but it was too late for me to stop." She paused to get herself together. "Ben, it was a girl."

"Oh no, Jacqueline!"

"Yeah, and it gets worse. Do you remember what I told you the other day about the girl who set me up with the stolen car and packet of cocaine?"

"Sure, what was her name? Shelby?"

"Yes." She bit her lip to hold back tears and then continued. "She was the girl lying in the street."

"Holy shit! Oh, sorry. I didn't mean to curse, but wow, is she okay?"

She shook her head. "She didn't make it. The injuries were fatal. I went to her while I waited for the ambulance. I saw her injuries. I think she was almost decapitated. It was horrible!" Her hands were shaking as she attempted to pour the coffee. She handed the carafe to Ben. "Would you mind? I'm afraid I'll spill it all over. I'm just simply devastated about this. I cannot get the image of her lying there—bleeding and dying—out of my mind. It was by far one of the worst things that I've ever had to witness and it was all my fault."

"I can only imagine. Jackie, I am so sorry."

He got up to embrace her and she fought back the tears. As they both sat down, she told him the rest.

"There's more, though." She paused to gauge a reaction. She was afraid that Ben was going to take off running out of the house and never look back. When he sat still and didn't bolt for the door, she continued. "The other part of this story is that there is a detective who questioned me in the hospital. He played it off as proper procedure—at first. After my parents left the room, he badgered me a bit harder, as if he wanted me to confess that I did this on purpose. He spoke to me like I was some kind of insane criminal under investigation. Can you imagine?"

"What? That is preposterous! I haven't even known you for that long and I can vouch that you would never do that. He actually said that? He came straight out and accused you?"

"No, but he didn't have to. I almost wish that he did, though, so I could defend myself."

"You said you were in the hospital? Were you hurt or did you go to be with Shelby?"

"No, I wasn't hurt. Well, not really, anyway. I passed out when I realized the extent of Shelby's injuries. I was horrified when I saw her lifeless body. I never saw anything like that in my life. It was surreal. It's an image I don't think I can ever forget. I wish I could just erase it like chalk." She closed her eyes as if that would permanently wipe away the image. "Anyway, he didn't accuse me. It was the way he looked at me and the type of questions he asked. I couldn't help myself. At first I was afraid, then that fear turned to infuriation. I yelled at him before I left. I couldn't stand it anymore. I'm quite certain he'll try to hold that against me. He'll probably try to tell me I have an anger management issue. Who knows?"

"So, what happens next? Do you have to go to court? Did they mention whether they are they going to charge you or not?"

"To be completely honest, I don't know. I don't think so. They have my car for more "routine" tests, I guess to see if there is any evidence of drugs or alcohol, even though they gave me a blood test last night. They said I'll get the car back within a week. For all I care, they can keep it. I know every time I climb into it, I'm going to relive the nightmare of last night."

"Yeah, I have to admit, I'm pretty sure that I'd feel the same way. Did they mention if they are doing an autopsy? I mean, what was she doing in the middle of the street, anyway? Didn't they find that sort of peculiar?"

"Yep, they are, but it could take anywhere from a week to a month."

"I don't know what to say. I'm so sorry."

"Me too. I feel awful about it."

"Well, if there's anything I can do to take your mind off of it, let me know. This may sound inappropriate, but do you want to get out of the house for a while, maybe take a walk? It may be good just to give yourself something else to focus on."

"I'm not sure, not just yet. Not that I don't want to, but yesterday was just a weird day right from the beginning. Can I take a rain check? I think I need some time to myself to get my thoughts together."

"Did something else happen yesterday? I hope you're not referring to our date?" He gave an impish smile, trying to lighten the mood.

"Didn't I tell you who installed my water heater?"

"No, I don't believe that you mentioned it last night. "

"I didn't want to think about it. Do you remember there was another kid that was involved the night of the car theft?" She sighed. "The person who came to install the heater was none other than him—Montgomery. It was as if my past came back to haunt me, all in one day. If I had seen Chad, the third kid involved in my arrest, I would really be paranoid right about now. I don't think I can handle any more. To add insult to injury, he showed up at the hospital as I was leaving. I guess him and Shelby were still friends or maybe more." Recalling what she'd seen in Montgomery's van, she felt sickened all over again. She contemplated telling Ben, but refrained. She didn't know him well enough, even though they had been spending a lot of time together and he seemed supportive. She didn't want him to think she was going crazy. Anyway, it was possible that she was overreacting about the blood in the van.

"That is strange! What a bizarre coincidence, huh?"

"Definitely."

"To say you had an interesting day is an understatement." He sipped his coffee as if trying to decipher the next course of action. Part of him wanted to convince her to get out and take her mind off of things, but the other part of him realized that she probably needed some time to herself. "Okay, well, take all the time that you need. If you want to chat, cry, vent, or just sit there and stare at my pitiful mug, come on by. My door is open for you."

She mustered a laugh and gave him a hug. "Thanks, Ben. I might just do that. My parents are supposed to lend me one of their cars, so I might just go for a drive later. Perhaps after that, I'll stop by."

"Sounds good. I'll be here. If I'm not, just call my cell phone, okay?"

"Yes, thanks again."

"No problem, and Jacqueline?"

"Yeah?"

"I read a quote once in a magazine that seems apropos for what you are going through. I remember it whenever bad things happen in my life: 'Bad things sometimes happen to good people. Don't let the tragedies of yesterday ruin the promise of today.'"

"Well, that is profound. I'm going to have to commit that to memory!"

She managed to smile now. In the midst of everything that had happened, she was thankful that she had at least made a friend.

"It's very true. Remember, call me if you need me."

"Will do."

Chapter 15: Paranoia

Shortly after Ben left, Jacqueline's parents arrived, each driving a separate car so that they would be able to leave one with their daughter.

"Thanks so much for coming," she said.

"You're our daughter," replied her father. "Of course we'd come! We know it was an accident, Jackie. You mustn't blame yourself for things that are out of your control. Sometimes the world hands out impossible situations; how you handle them makes all of the difference."

"Thanks, Dad. I know what you're saying."

"What do you say that we all go out to lunch?" her mother suggested. "Get our minds off of this terrible tragedy?"

"Thanks, Mom, but if you guys don't mind, I'd like some time by myself. Please don't take offense. I know it sounds silly, but I need some alone time. I want to get my mind wrapped around this whole thing. It's not only the accident, it's Shelby as a person."

"That's fine, honey," said her father. "Listen, I know a few people in the coroner's office, and a couple of the medical examiners owe me a favor. I've already spoken to them, and I'm going to get them to do an autopsy first thing." Hoping to cheer her up just a little, he gave her the rest of the news. "We should have the results before this week is through. It may help you to know that they believe Shelby was on drugs. Keep that to yourself, but that's how it appears. You might not have been responsible after all. She might have already been dead."

"Dad, while that may take the blame off me, it's still a life that was wasted. Do you know what I mean? Where was her family? How did they let that happen to her? It's those thoughts I need to iron out. I promise. I'm fine. You don't have to keep trying to make me feel better. I'll call you tonight."

"Okay. You win. Call us if you need anything."

"I will."

"And be careful. You're not in your right mind and there are so many crazies out there. They're like scavengers, seeking out vulnerability."

"I know, Dad. I'll be careful and I'm in my right mind. It just happens to be tangled right now." She mustered a smile.

Once her parents were well out of sight, Jacqueline got in the car and drove around aimlessly. Though she didn't smoke frequently, she did every now and then. This seemed as good a time as any to light up.

Before she knew it, she had been driving all over the island for an hour only to end up at the beach, twenty minutes away from her house. She parked in a corner and noticed only two other cars parked. Another pulled up behind her, but drove to the opposite side of the lot.

With the car windows open, she lit up another cigarette and rested her head back on the seat. Gazing out at the limitless ocean gave her the lift that she needed and the inspiration to get her thoughts together. She thought about the quote that Ben had recited to her and then remembered another one she had read last week in a women's magazine: *There's a whole world out there. Only you can make the choice to embrace it. Dare to be empowered!*

She repeated the last line and snickered. *Dare to be empowered.* She had never felt less empowered in her life.

After a few more moments, she turned her key in the ignition and headed back toward home. Shortly after she departed the parking lot, the same car that had pulled in behind her left, too, and a frothing wave of nervousness tumbled through her mind. If she didn't know any better, she'd swear that she was being followed. The car kept its distance, but remained directly behind her.

After a moment, the other two cars left the lot as well. She looked up to see the clouds in the sky and realized they were only leaving at the same time to avoid the upcoming storm.

I'm such an idiot. No one's following me. It's just my father's protective voice of doom filling my thoughts.

Once she pulled off the highway, the first car remained closely behind her, but made a left onto one of the side streets.

See, he wasn't following you.

She pulled into her driveway and Ben was outside his house, pruning some of his trees before the rain. "Hey stranger! How are you feeling?" he called.

Pleased to see him, she exited her car and walked across the street to his house. "Good, much better now. Just needed to clear my mind. Still got some stubborn cobwebs taking up space, but I cleared away some of them and put things into their proper compartments."

"That's great. Hopefully it helps you stay focused. Are you hungry by any chance?"

"Well…now that you mentioned it, yes. Come to think of it, I haven't eaten all day."

"I didn't think so. I made some lasagna and was waiting for someone to eat it with me. Interested?"

"Since you twisted my arm, how can I possibly say no?"

"Great, come on in. Let me just get cleaned up. Go inside and make yourself comfortable! It looks like a storm is heading our way."

As she walked in, she couldn't help but smile. His house was immaculate, but showed every trace of being a stereotypical bachelor pad. Framed pieces of art hung in the living room, displaying a variety of polished automobiles. His video game system was bundled neatly in the entertainment center, along with a vast selection of popular games. As he returned to the living room, he caught her eyeing it.

"Do you play?"

"Oh my, you startled me."

"I seem to do that a lot to you, don't I?"

"Yes! And, yes, I do actually."

"Which games?"

"Any of them. I love video games."

"Awesome! Now I have someone to play with!"

Laughing now, she said, "You sound like a five-year old."

"In here, I definitely am one." He pointed to his heart. "What do you say we eat? I'm starving."

"Yeah, me too. I think that's my stomach growling."

"Good thing. I thought there might be a dog that I didn't know I had."

"Ha ha, very funny."

The conversation was free of awkward silence as they sat down to dinner. It all felt very comfortable and to Jacqueline, very necessary. She enjoyed the distraction, as well as his company.

"So, how was your drive? Go anywhere special?"

"Nah, I just drove around a bit, went down to the beach, and admired the water."

"That's good. Sometimes your brain needs detoxification. The beach is the perfect spot for that. There's something about miles upon miles of water to put the mind in a state of relaxation."

She chuckled. "Yeah, I actually got myself a little worked up. For a brief moment I thought someone was following me, but it was just my father's voice of concern ringing through my ears as always. My imagination playing eternal tricks on me."

"Do you have enemies I should know about?" he joked. She knew he would do anything to remove the sinister cloud hanging over her head; he must hate to see her so solemn and glum.

"No. Well, not really."

"Uh-oh."

"No, other than that every once in a while I worry that Terrance is going to come here and bother me."

"Your ex-boyfriend, Terrance? This may be out of line, but was he abusive to you?"

"Terrance?" She nearly choked on her drink. "Oh, no. He was never abusive, at least not to me. He was actually a very sweet, but possessive, person. We had what you might call a bad breakup. He was very clingy, so when I wanted to end it with him, he called every chance that he got."

"Clingy, huh?"

"Yeah, he stopped by my parents' house a few times, but my father finally stepped in and had a talk with him—man-to-man, as my father would say."

"Ah. Your dad showed him who's boss."

"I suppose. After that, he didn't really come around too often, but the phone calls didn't stop. He begged me to come back to him. He didn't understand what he did wrong. You know how that goes."

"So, what *did* he do wrong?" Ben seemed to like listening to her speak. She loosened up a little when she did, and the frown lines disappeared from her forehead a bit.

"That's just it. He was clingy. I couldn't breathe. I loved having a boyfriend, but I also loved being alone. He needed me for everything. After a while, it became exhausting."

"Oh, yeah, I see your point. I wouldn't be able to deal, either."

"Exactly."

"So, did he ever follow you before to make you worry now?"

"Just once. Well, I only caught him once. I stopped short and got out. I was having a bad day and I couldn't stand it. I yelled at him, like one of those crazy ladies you see getting arrested on television. Afterwards, I felt bad. He didn't know what hit him. Neither did I, to be honest. My throat was killing me after all of that screaming!" Ben was smirking now, as if envisioning her making a public scene. "I haven't seen him since. Either he's moved on, or he's just more careful to avoid any path I might be on."

"I think you probably scared him half to death. The poor guy was shaking in his boots. Remind me not to mess with you on a bad day!"

She winked as she retorted, "Consider yourself warned."

As they finished their meal, they each took their wine glasses and moseyed to the wicker loveseat in the center of the backyard. Though the sky was threatening, no drops of moisture had yet fallen. The winds started to pick up and the branches swayed, causing a few stray buds to fall to the ground.

Not normally a lush, Jacqueline decided she could do whatever she pleased tonight. She'd been through hell and back, and the guilt from yesterday's accident was haunting her.

"Tell me, dear Jacqueline."

"Oh, so proper!" His smile made her blush. She was falling for him. Hard.

"Why, when I brought up dating, did you shy away from it? It doesn't sound like Terrance was all that bad of a guy. Clingy yes, but not terrible."

Feeling a little tipsy from the wine, she was a little less reserved. "Well, to be honest, I thought all guys might be as dependent as Terrance."

"And now?" He inched a little closer so that they were face-to-face. He could feel her breath and inched in a little more.

"Well, um, I'm not so sure."

His eyes danced when they locked with hers, resulting in a dizzying trance when she returned his gaze. Their conversation came to an abrupt stop, sealed with a long awaited—and most welcomed—kiss. When they came up for air, Ben simply smiled. "See, I'm not so bad, am I?"

Utterly speechless, she forced herself to say something, anything, that would get rid of her ridiculous grin. "No, I guess you're not."

Holding her hands in his, he said, "I'd like for you to give me a chance. Just one chance. If it is too much for you, then I'll back off and we can remain friends. There are no strings attached." He held out his hands as if he were flicking crumbs from his fingertips. "See? No strings. I won't even follow you in my car. I may, however, follow you down the driveway. Maybe peek in your windows."

That did it. She was finally laughing. "Okay, you win!"

"Yes!" he joked. "More wine?"

"Sure, another glass couldn't hurt."

They spent part of the night together, waiting for the storm and sipping wine. When it started to get late, Jacqueline said she had to leave.

"You're truly going to leave me? Please stay!" She gave him one stare that said all that needed to be said. "Okay, I get it. Let me at least walk you to your house."

"All right, I'll make an exception and let you do that."

Their night ended with a sweet kiss on the front porch.

"See you tomorrow?" This time it was *her* that was asking for a date.

"Wow, definitely! With bells on!"

"Um, you can keep the bells off. How about breakfast at my place at eight a.m.?"

"I'll bring the bagels."

"I look forward to it."

Chapter 16: Butter

The guilt of taking the life of another human being still weighed heavily on Jacqueline's mind, but she realized now that if it hadn't been her to seal Shelby's fate, then it would have been another unsuspecting soul.

Feeling a bit drowsy from the wine, she set her security alarm and crawled into bed. She didn't think she would need the anti-anxiety medication tonight, nor did she want to mix it with the wine, but she kept it on her nightstand just in case. To her pleasant surprise, she fell asleep instantly.

She dreamt that she was at a park with Ben. They had been together for a long time and had known each other since childhood. They had the kind of trust one would feel in a long-term relationship.

It was a sunny day, but the clouds warned of an upcoming storm, covering the orange sunlight every few minutes with puffy onyx clouds. Jacqueline's hair was cut short and she was running through the park, Ben following closely behind. They set a checkered picnic blanket down and got ready to dig in to the basket that held their food and beverages.

Once they took a seat on the blanket, out of nowhere a young golden retriever appeared and ran up to them like he had known them his entire life. In his mouth, he held a sneaker with the laces dangling from either side, and attached to his collar was a well-chewed tennis ball. It was easy to tell that he fancied a wide assortment of toys and had selected the two that were his favorites. His owners must have attached the tennis ball to his collar for safekeeping. Jacqueline looked at his name tag. "Butter" was imprinted across the top, but no address was engraved beneath it.

The friendly dog lay down next to them for a while, panting and sneaking a drink out of their plastic picnic glasses every now and then, and closely watching the flock of birds that flew directly overhead, but making no attempt to run after them.

When the clouds started getting darker, the dog jumped into Jacqueline's lap and stared intently into her eyes. At first she thought he was afraid of the rain, as so many dogs are, but the intensity of his stare proved otherwise. She felt a strong emotion, like nothing she had ever felt before. It was as if she had the ability to see directly into his soul, and he was giving her some kind of a message—warning her to be careful.

He then jumped off of her lap, grabbed his sneaker, and ran into the direction from which he came. She noticed there were dozens and dozens of dogs waiting for him, and he gave one final bark and a wag of his tail before disappearing behind the trees.

She looked toward Ben, but he had disappeared as well. The beautiful park became dismal and lonely, like an enchanted forest that had been tainted with dread. The trees disappeared and then her entire world was black. As she rose up from the blanket to run out of the park, she heard a faint sound: *Intruder, intruder. Your security has been breached. Warning, there is an intruder.*

Gasping for air, Jacqueline jumped out of bed awoken from her dream. She knew the alarm would send out a blaring signal ten seconds after the initial breach, and then her telephone should ring. When the unit had been installed, the technician had tested it, and it was much louder than what she was hearing right now. Her breath caught in her throat as she waited for the continuation of the alarm to sound.

An intruder had entered her home. Terror temporarily crippled her as she stood by her bed, waiting for what seemed like eternity.

Nothing happened. No second warning. No phone call from central station. No loud alarm.

More frightened than she had ever been in her life, she ripped the plug out of the wall, wrapping her trembling hands around the wooden lamp that she had just purchased earlier that week from a rustic store outside of town. Her palms felt like sopping sponges and her heart thrummed like a rabid bat in a tiny cage.

Fearing for her life, she peeked out of her bedroom door and saw the light from the kitchen. She tried to remember if she had left it on when she went to sleep earlier. Or did the intruder turn it on? She then remembered she had indulged in a little too much cabernet. What she had done before bedtime was a complete blur.

As she rounded the corner, she noted it was not the kitchen light, but the dim illumination from the night-light, which she always left on. She wanted nothing more than to feel relief, but she wasn't out of the woods yet. Someone could be lurking right behind her.

A slight trickle of air tickled her neck. She spun around, the lamp in her hand, and searched the shadows for her prowler, a scream getting ready to dislodge from her throat.

In the living room, something moved. She felt someone's eyes on her. In her peripheral vision, a black object passed by, but when she turned around, she saw no one.

Now completely sober, she knew she had to fight or flee. She just didn't know if she could escape fast enough. Shadows dangled on the walls like tiny puppets in some obscene show, their shark-like jaws getting ready to swallow her whole.

Fumbling to get to the phone, she lifted the receiver, her eyes peeled for the trespasser—but he seemed to have disappeared.

She wondered why central station still hadn't called. With the lamp still in her right hand, she pushed the buttons for 911 with her left.

A nasally operator answered. She used to wonder if they were all trained to sound exactly alike. Right now, she didn't care; she only wanted help.

"Nine-one-one. What is the nature of your emergency?"

"There's an intruder. Fourteen Birchwood Street. Hacamatac Terrace. Come quickly!" she whispered into the phone loud enough for the operator to hear, but she hoped, her intruder could not.

She left the phone off of the hook in case 911 was recording the call. If the intruder managed to attack Jacqueline, at least the operator would be able to hear exactly what was happening and expedite assistance. She screamed at the top of her lungs, hoping the intruder would scare easily and a neighbor, possibly Ben, would hear her. "Okay, whoever you are! The police are coming. You can leave now. I haven't even seen you yet. I can't identify you. Please leave now!"

As she moved through the house, she carefully tiptoed. She wanted to turn on the light in each room as she passed by, as if illumination would shield her from danger. She was now in view of the front door, able to see the alarm pad. On it, the steady glow of the red light was solid. She remembered that once the alarm had been tripped, it would blink red.

Her first instinct was to protect her castle, but realized there was a chance she might not be alive long enough to do so. So when logic kicked in, she quietly opened the front door, feeling that she'd be safer outside, near witnesses and a possible chance to run. But as she turned the handle, she found that it was locked. How was that possible? With frenzied urgency, she unlocked it and pulled the door toward her, shocked by the resonant blast of the alarm.

Stunned, she jumped and dropped the lamp, shattering tiny light bulb pieces all over the floor.

Intruder, intruder. Your security has been breached. The computerized voice repeated itself, and after ten seconds, the alarm blasted once more, loud enough to be heard from down the block and presumably into the next town. Relieved to still be alive, she jumped onto her front step.

Her telephone rang. She ignored the call. The police were already on their way. She was afraid to go back into the house and terrified to be by herself.

Seeing Ben's light flicker on, she ran over there and banged on his door. Within seconds, he opened it and her body collapsed into her arms.

"Jackie, is everything okay?"

"I don't know, Ben. I'm confused. I don't know what happened. I think there was an intruder, but now I'm not so sure. I think I might have dreamt it."

"What? Your alarm is blasting."

"I know, but oh my goodness. The cops are on their way." Her normal levelheadedness seemed to have disappeared.

"Jacqueline, of course someone tripped your alarm! How else would it have gone off?"

Hanging her head in shame, Jacqueline began to think she had lost her mind. "I set it off! I thought I heard it go off. I was sleeping. It was really low, but I could have sworn I heard the alarm. That's when I called the cops. Then I opened the front door—I just felt safer outside—but no one was ever really there. It was still locked. Ben, I must have dreamt it! There's no other explanation." Her face switched back and forth from too pale to scarlet red, as if she had seen a ghost but had then become embarrassed by its improbability.

"Okay, calm down. Let the cops check out your house and your property. We'll straighten this all out."

Just as they took a step toward her house, the police cars came zipping around the corner with their lights flashing. The first officer exited his car and approached her and Ben. "Are you the person who called?"

"Yes, I'm Jacqueline."

"Is this your house?"

"Yes."

"Did you report an intruder?"

"Yes, I did, but officer…" Her voice trailed off as another cop exited the vehicle. Ben grabbed her arm as if to warn her.

"Dirks, let's check around back, then we'll go into the house."

Within minutes, they returned. "All clear."

"Ma'am, did you say he escaped?"

Exasperated and embarrassed, she did what she could to clear up the situation, although the cops were growing more confused by the minute. "No, officers, I'm sorry for the disturbance. I thought I heard my alarm go off. I…I guess I was dreaming."

The two officers shared a private look. One started to speak and realized it was a lost cause. "Okay, well, if that's all, just sign this police report and we'll be on our way."

"I'm sorry, officers, truly I am."

"It's okay...this time. Please be more cognizant of your situation next time."

"I will, I promise."

Lately, Jacqueline thought, she seemed to be forever pushing doors marked "pull." She turned to Ben. "One minute things are going great, the next, I run over my archenemy, and everything goes south from there. Any time there is turmoil in my life, Shelby is the one behind it." Jacqueline had just unleashed the devil on her shoulder. She didn't need a mirror to look at her own reflection; she could see it just by watching Ben. "Oh my goodness. I can't believe I just said that. I didn't mean that."

"It's okay."

"No, it's not okay, Ben! The girl is dead. She's dead because I killed her—accident or not. And yet here I go running my mouth about how she is the root of all of my problems." Ben only listened as, like an old tea kettle that has reached its boiling point, she continued to blow off steam. "It's just that during any part of my life that has gone off track, Shelby was part of it. The kicker is that she and I were not even great friends. I met her at a party, we seemed to have a lot in common, and I think we hung out a total of three times before she got me arrested. Yet, here I am feeling a mountain of incessant guilt over ending her life. I shouldn't have said what I said, but I am so frustrated, I want to scream!"

"Listen, let's mosey on into your house before we wake the neighborhood. My Irish mother always used to make tea when things went awry, so I'll put on a kettle while you relax on the couch."

"No, you don't have to do that. I'm sorry I'm a little crazy right now. I swear to you, I am not normally like this."

"That's okay. It's kind of sexy, especially since you still have bedhead."

"Oh my god! I didn't even brush my hair. The cops saw me like this! You too! I can't believe this!"

As Ben smirked, Jacqueline did her best to smooth out any stray strands. Red-faced and distraught, she ran into the house and into to the bathroom to fix herself up. When she came back, Ben was sitting at the kitchen table with two cups of tea set out for them, and a box of chocolate doughnuts he had found in her cupboard.

"Did I mention that you look beautiful?"

"Oh, shut up!" She tried to appear angry, but grabbed a doughnut and tried to ignore Ben's remarks.

He had to tease her just a little. "Ya know, the alarm thing was no big deal, but, I really can't believe you didn't fix your hair. I mean, I know there was this big bad intruder and all, but you couldn't take a second to look in the mirror first before defending your domicile? Sheesh, what kind of a woman are you?"

Feeling a little bit like her old self, she retorted with sarcasm. "What kind of woman am I? A very tired, cranky, stressed and, at the moment, psychotic woman. One who thinks you may want to retract your last statement before this cup of hot tea accidentally finds itself poured over your head. That's the type of woman I am."

Enjoying the banter, Ben pretended to back off. "Whoa, sorry, woman! I forgot who I was dealing with."

She flashed one of her sexiest winks at him. "Just don't ever forget again."

"Wooeee! Your hair looks beautiful, Jackie. Don't ever change a thing."

"Thin ice, Ben!"

"What? I'm being serious. Can't I compliment you?"

"Sure, just not tonight." She couldn't help but smirk at her flippant attitude, and nudged Ben so he'd know she was kidding. Though the last few days had been stressful, she didn't want to ruin what she had going with her new friend. He was way too interesting to let go.

As they finished their tea and doughnuts, Jacqueline yawned and stretched. "I think I have to go to sleep, Ben. I can't even see straight."

"Okay, do you want me to stay?"

"Um, yes, but that's okay. If you stay tonight, I may never want you to leave."

They both exchanged lingering glances before he nodded and walked to the front door, and he managed to give her a kiss that she knew she would remember. Knowing that he was doing his best to get permission to stay the night, Jacqueline kissed him back before sending him on his way.

Thunder cracked in the sky and the long-awaited rain finally began splattering to the ground in a torrential storm that was relentless and even damaging. In her heart, Jacqueline wanted nothing more than for Ben to stay but felt that she needed to be able to stay alone. This was her home. This was where she was supposed to feel safe. No one was going to take that from her.

Feeling a bit better, she washed dishes in the sink, put them away, and then wiped down the countertops as well. Before heading to her bedroom, she glanced outside the window into the black of night. "What the...?"

A lump caught in her throat as she watched a figure run through her backyard. She was unable to see clearly with the rain coming down, but she knew she wasn't seeing things. It looked like, running alongside the pool, was a man dressed in black from head to toe. But there were too many large trees around her yard to differentiate between them, and it was possible that it wasn't a person at all. The way the wind was blowing, she reasoned, it might have only looked like a moving figure, someone running with a pole-like object in hand.

She rubbed her eyes and peeked out again, this time turning off the lights in order to get a better look. She inhaled and didn't release her breath for a long moment, but she saw nothing but the trees swaying in the wind and the downpour falling from the sky. The running figure had been a figment of her imagination, again exposing her mind for what it was—delirious. But as her head hit the pillow, she couldn't help but think that the ominous figure had looked very real.

She was going to need her anti-anxiety medication after all.

Chapter 17: Awareness

The vibration of her cell phone on the nightstand woke Jacqueline out of her already-interrupted sleep.

"Hiya, honey! Guess what?"

Her voice still groggy, she was less than enthusiastic. "Oh, I dunno, Dad, you had way too much coffee this morning?"

"Not quite enough. I only had three cups. I've got some good news for you. It will bring you out of that awful depression that you are slipping into."

"Unless the news is that I can go back to sleep, I don't see how good it is going to be. And just to set things straight, I'm not depressed. I'm just having a difficult time coming to terms with what happened."

"Well, we got the autopsy report back as I promised I would. See? It helps to know people in high places." Never one to be modest, her father had no problem boasting when warranted.

"Yes, yes, I suppose it does. Well, now that you've got my full attention, what did the autopsy report say? Let me guess, the victim died from getting hit by a car?"

Ignoring her, he continued. "The preliminary reports show that she had a heart attack. While that might not have killed her if help had come along, it definitely placed her a foot in the grave."

"Dad! Please, that's horrible to say!"

"I didn't mean for it to sound so heartless, but they believe that she also overdosed, Jacqueline. The centers of her arms had track marks and black-and-blues. They believe she was shooting heroin."

"Well, that makes sense."

"See what I mean? The police report officially recorded the incident as an accident. They'll have the rest of the report in two to three weeks, but I can promise you that they are not bringing you up on charges. Anyone driving down that road wouldn't have seen her. It was way too dark." She listened while he went on. "If she overdosed, and I have no doubt that she did, I'm sure we are going to find that the dose was lethal and would've caused a person of Shelby's build to collapse. If you hadn't come along when you did, most likely Shelby would've died later that evening from her own doing. I hate to sound so abrupt, but that girl didn't stand a chance."

Her father gave Jacqueline the rest of the news. Since Shelby no longer had a family, no one had stepped up to press charges or take legal action against Jacqueline. While it was a relief from a legal standpoint, she couldn't help but feel traumatized still. She had too gentle a heart.

In addition, she couldn't understand how someone could get so hooked on cocaine and heroin. She had to imagine that during some time in Shelby's life she had had a loving and caring family. Where were they now? Had they disowned her? Jacqueline had never known the real Shelby. "I guess that's good news, Dad, but I still can't help but feel somewhat responsible, regardless of what Shelby did to me."

"Jacqueline, there was nothing you could've done. You didn't force her to take drugs, and if she hadn't gotten you arrested when she did, we all know that you would've been kind enough to try to help her."

"Dad, I guess sometimes people can't help it. They get hooked. I realize it was her decision to take drugs in the first place, but it's still a shame. The entire situation leaves me feeling a bit sickened."

"Yes, you're right. It is a shame, but there's nothing you could've done. Stop beating yourself up over it. I know emotionally, this bothers you, but if you can see the bright side of things for one moment, legally you are off the hook."

"Yeah, but not if Detective Brown has anything to say about it."

"Don't worry about him."

"Don't worry about him? Dad, did you hear him? I'm pretty sure he was ready to read me the riot act. He knew about my past history with Shelby and thought this was some delayed act of revenge. You heard the way he was talking to me in the hospital, reviewing the notes on his little clipboard like I was going to 'fess up to some malicious hate crime."

"Well, he can't prove anything now. It was an accident. Free and clear. There's nothing he can do about it."

"I guess. God forbid I get a little traffic violation. He's going to be watching me like a hawk."

"It'll blow over, Jacqueline. He's probably come to his senses by now. He's got bad guys to catch. You're one of the good guys."

"I suppose. Well, thanks for the news, Dad. I need to make myself a cup of coffee and wake up a little."

"No problem. You can have your car back by the end of this week."

'Yeah, about that. I think I'm going to sell it. I can't drive it knowing what happened. I feel like it is tainted. Every time I get in, I'm going to be reminded of Shelby's awful death."

"Well, it's up to you. Make sure that you think it through. If you still don't want it, let me know if you need my help selling it."

"Will do." Jacqueline plopped her head back onto the pillow. At least she wasn't going to be brought up on charges. That would've been the icing on this tasteless, multi-layer cake.

She had one more day to get herself together before she returned to work, so she figured she might as well get up and get moving. *Try to stay out of trouble today, Jackie.*

Once she was finished getting ready, she got in her parents' car and drove out to run errands. She called Ben on his cell phone to let him know she had to delay their morning plans and would call him when she got home.

With the music blasting, she opened her windows and sung each song on the radio to her heart's content, hoping that no one would be able to hear her ear-piercing voice. She knew her singing probably sounded like a wounded cow, but it was a good release.

Though she was driving the speed limit, the car behind her was tailgating. In an effort to avoid any type of drama today, she switched lanes and allowed him to pass. To her surprise, the driver of the car switched lanes behind her. With her sunglasses on, she peeked in the rearview mirror to get a good look at the person behind the wheel. She couldn't quite see his eyes, since he also had on sunglasses and a black cap. He swerved when she swerved and mirrored her every move.

Okay, now I'm hallucinating. Why would someone be tailgating me? Though she tried to dissuade herself from thinking morbid thoughts, she was growing increasingly aggravated. She was also exhausted.

Unsure of how to proceed, she pulled into the shopping center in a feeble attempt to lose him. To her pleasant surprise, the driver kept going and sped away.

What is happening to me?

When she got out of her car, her legs staggered like she had had one too many drinks, and she paused a moment to allow her lungs to exhale. She leaned over, using the hood of the car to steady her equilibrium and regain her balance. Once she felt she was in the clear, she tucked her hair behind her ear, grabbed her purse and her keys, and ventured into the store.

Just your damn imagination, Jacqueline. No one's following you.

The mind has a way of playing tricks, and at that particular moment, Jacqueline's was like a magician carrying a top hat and a fluffy white rabbit. Throw a black cape and a wand into the mix, she thought, and you'd have real entertainment.

The past few days she had exercised her imagination to its fullest extent, conjuring up scenarios that only made sense to her —a phantom intruder, a car following her at the beach, and now this.

Perhaps the driver today just never passed his road test and drives like an imbecile. Wouldn't that seem more rational?

She waited a moment before heading into the store, watching as a man who appeared to be in a rush, and hiding himself from the world, walked to his car carrying a vase of roses. He then walked back from his car—this time with a cowboy hat covering his head—into the store, walking much slower, more confidently, and obviously more relaxed. Noting that the only difference from when she first had first seen him walking was the cowboy hat, she wondered if she should go and buy one. Maybe that would turn her luck around.

Running in her direction was a pack of children. They reminded her of wild animals, the way they were screaming and carrying on. She glanced over their heads in search of their parents and finally spotted the mother, talking on her cell phone and not paying attention as the youngest of the children ran directly in front of a moving car.

"Watch out!" Jacqueline's scream saved the child's life. The driver stopped short just in time, rolled down his window, and yelled at both the kid and at her mother. He then was cordial enough to thank Jacqueline. The mother, on the other hand, barely showed a reaction and kept yapping away like nothing had ever happened.

It figures. She had already taken more than she could handle, and if she had witnessed another horrific accident, she would have lost it. While she wanted to scream at the mother for not paying attention, she only managed to shoot her a dirty look.

Okay. You came here for a purpose. Get going. The nagging voice inside her head forced her to take charge.

She walked into the department store, at first looking over her shoulder and then relaxing once she got inside.

She browsed aimlessly through the racks and found that she was enjoying herself quite a bit. After trying on a plethora of different outfits, she settled on a few and walked to the counter to ring them up. Her mind was floating elsewhere, not even noticing the person standing behind her. If she had, she might have recognized him.

Chapter 18: Uncertainty

It had been three full days since Donovan had heard from Carmine. There'd been no news about Montgomery's demise or even how or where his partner had disposed of the kid's body. There had been no nervous phone calls, no checking in with the business—in short, not a word.

It wasn't unlike Carmine, as there had been many instances where he had gone on drug-filled excursions into distant lands of irresponsibility and hadn't shown up for days at a time. This type of holiday was common for him, Donovan thought, and was most likely the case now. Carmine had most likely killed Montgomery in a remote location where no one had heard the shots. Once the deed was done, he had probably rummaged through Montgomery's pockets looking for the one sweet thing to fulfill his burning desire—cocaine. Since Friday had been both payday and the day that Carmine had been supposed to escort Montgomery out of this world, it was likely that dear Monty had had a nice stash tucked neatly in his jean pockets, or at least in the inner lining of his sweatshirt. Wherever it was, Carmine would have found it, and if lucky, a sizable wad of cash as well. He would have been ecstatic, especially since the cash would have come from their own stolen property.

Still, Donovan couldn't shake the feeling that something was terribly wrong. While Carmine had never been responsible, killing someone was still a big deal. It had often taken less than that to rattle Carmine's fragile nerves, and he would have at least felt the need to at least check in with Donovan. It was doubtful that his conscience was *so* spoiled that he didn't even feel an ounce of guilt—or paranoia. Did he not even need to talk about it, and share how it all went down? Donovan's concern quickly metamorphosed to anger and disgust. *If nothing else, did that selfish son-of-a-bitch not have the decency to share whatever he found with me? I'll kill him if he hoarded all of the good stuff for himself. Does he think he's the only freaking one who's stressed?*

He didn't even realize there were customers in the shop when he kicked a stack of PVC piping and punched a hole in the wall. "Shit!"

"Um, hello?"

"Oh, sorry, ma'am. I just tripped over my own clumsy feet and made a mess back there. I didn't know anyone was out here, I'm sorry."

"That's okay. I hope you didn't hurt yourself too badly."

"No, no nothing like that. I'm used to being a klutz. How can I help you?"

His eyes were squeezed into tiny slits and his jaw tight. He did his best to soften his gaze as he conversed with his client.

"I need to have someone come to my house and fix my ice-maker; the water is not flowing to it. It makes this annoying buzzing sound, like a drunken bee." While Donovan pulled himself together, the customer kept speaking. "I would have called, but I couldn't find the number and I was just passing by. Do you have a business card or something?"

"Sure. I, uh, I could have someone there tomorrow. We're a bit short-staffed today. And, here's a card." He reached into the open drawer of the desk and pulled out his own card. It was seated right next to his gun, which he pushed back out of sight.

"Oh, okay. Do you know what time you will be arriving?"

"I can be there between eight and ten. Is that okay with you?"

"Sure. I'll be home."

Donovan took down her information and realized he couldn't depend on Carmine to show up. This realization ignited his rage once again, like white, burning flames in a forest blaze. *Great. I have one employee who is floating face down at the bottom of the ocean and another one who is as good as dead. I guess it will all depend on me then.*

Then he looked at the stack of papers he had Carmine sign before he left the other day, and smiled. *I guess I made the right decision after all.*

Chapter 19: Clarification

Donovan pulled himself together and started working on the bookkeeping, formulating his next plan of action. But his concentration got interrupted at about nine-fifteen, when he heard the rumble of tires on the pavement outside. He looked up from his paperwork to see one of the work vans pull up—the van that Carmine had left in a few days prior.

Well, well, well. The idiot decided to come to work after all. A fire burned inside of his belly as he punched his fist on the desk before getting up to greet Carmine at the front door. *Better the desk than your face, Carmine.*

He watched as the van's door opened, anticipating seeing his partner's haggard frown lines and slouched posture, but instead saw a skinny figure exit the driver's seat. He had too much pep in his step to be Carmine, and Donovan would recognize that worn black cap anywhere.

Donovan's face turned a bone-chilling white. He tried to mask his confusion by looking away, but there was nowhere else to divert his gaze.

"Hey boss."

Donovan's breathing became shallow as he looked behind him to see if anyone else was in the van. "Montgomery."

"Yeah, who were you expecting, Santa Claus?"

"What the hell are you doing with the work van? Only Carmine and me are to take that van home. You know that. Give me the damn keys."

Flipping the keys in air, Montgomery's smug demeanor and less-than-sparkling personality shone through. "Well, Carmine asked me to take it. You know how he is."

"Bullshit. He wouldn't dare do that. Where the hell is he?"

"Who?"

Getting angrier by the second and trying to disguise his uncertainty, Donovan grew impatient. Montgomery was supposed to be six feet under, yet here he was, alive as can be, while Carmine was nowhere to be found.

"Where the hell is Carmine, Montgomery?!" His voice amplified. In the pit of his stomach, he felt a flutter of butterflies, except these butterflies were carrying loaded weapons.

"How the heck am I supposed to know, Donnie?" The two men locked eyes. "Maybe Carmine is taking my car for a joyride. Funny how I left my car here on Friday, yet when I returned for it, it was gone. I found it at the pub down the street. Someone must have hotwired it, only to go two blocks and have a drink. That's pretty interesting, isn't it, Donnie?"

"Call me Donnie again and I'll make a permanent indentation in your face, Montgomery."

He was holding a hammer that he picked up off the counter upon seeing Montgomery's face. He didn't know why he picked it up or what he planned to do with it. He only knew that at that precise moment, he felt threatened. He also took solace in the fact that his gun was less than five feet away in his desk drawer. "I don't know why your car was at the bar. Are you sure you didn't go binge drinking and forget that you drove it there? You freaking waste of life!"

"Yeah, maybe that's it. Maybe I forgot. Sometimes it's easy to forget things, ya know? Like telling me we had a new security system. When was that put in?"

"None of your damn business. Get the hell out of here before I call the cops on your shoplifting ass. We saw the tapes, Montgomery. We know it was you. Do you have any questions, you piece of shit?"

"Questions? Hmm. Actually, I do—thanks for asking. Who the hell do you think you are talking to? Go ahead and call the cops, *Donnie*." He made sure to put emphasis on his name, watching his soon to be ex-boss get fired up, enjoying every minute of it. "Listen, I truly don't care what you do, Donnie. Why don't you do me a favor and tell Carmine I said good-bye when he gets here?" He winked at Donovan and followed it with a gripping, darkened stare that revealed everything Donovan needed to know.

He wouldn't have to worry about Carmine being late, paying his mortgage, going on a drug binge, or losing his temper. Carmine had never laid a hand on Montgomery. He had been outsmarted.

Chapter 20: Full Circle

While Donovan was astounded at the realization, in a portion of his heart, one neatly tucked away from the rest of the world, he couldn't help but feel a small sense of relief.

Some might say he should feel repentance about his partner being killed, but Donovan was amazed by his own keen sense of hindsight. Only two weeks prior to catching Montgomery on video, Donovan had discovered that the cash in his registers was way off balance. He had also noted that it was during the shifts when Carmine was the only one manning the shop. One Tuesday night, Carmine and Donovan had both gotten in their cars and driven home for the evening when Donovan then drove back and viewed the videotapes.

Sure enough, Carmine hadn't been the innocent partner that he had always claimed to be. As it turned out, Montgomery was not the only thief. Carmine had been helping himself to some extra cash when Donovan was out on field calls. Carmine's drug habit had been spiraling out of control, like a tiny car hydroplaning in a flash flood, and when Carmine was in need of a binge, he didn't think things through—like getting caught on camera.

When Donovan had handed Carmine the paperwork to sign last Friday, Carmine had failed to even read what he was agreeing to. Donovan lied and told him it was a lease renewal, but nothing could be further from the truth. The paperwork was an agreement to dissolve the business, agreeing to a seventy-thirty split of profits in Donovan's favor.

He couldn't believe how easy it was. At first, he wasn't even going to try to get away with it, but Carmine's temper had been lit like a blazing torch and it was the perfect opportunity for Donovan to seize. At the time, he had been vaguely concerned that Carmine would turn level-headed for a brief moment and actually read what he was signing, but it never happened.

Now that he thought about it, he wondered if Montgomery might have even done him a favor. Carmine's family wanted nothing to do with him, and they hadn't spoken in over fifteen years. They had disowned him due to his uncontrollable drug addiction and wouldn't even care that he was dead now. Donovan always paid Carmine's mortgage, and he was listed as a co-signor of the loan. He could legally sell the property with no questions asked. He might need to forge Carmine's signature, but that was easy. He could always pay one of his clients to act as a notary, if needed, since he knew plenty of people that were on the take. In Donovan's world, everyone could be bribed.

It was all coming together for him. His plan to retire at fifty was becoming less and less a dream and more and more a reality.

He supposed that he should feel slightly guilty that his old-time friend and partner had been murdered, but the truth was—he didn't. Not one bit. Their friendship had ended a long time ago when Carmine couldn't get his shit together. For a short time, Donovan had regretted that he hadn't been able to help him get on his feet, but he knew that no matter how he threatened him, drugs would always be more important. He slacked off at work, he stole, and he was blatantly rude and difficult. In fact, Carmine had been little more than deadweight for the past three years. Now, he was deadweight.

But where had Montgomery put the body, and would it somehow come back to haunt Donovan? Would anyone find out about his drug habit? He had enough incriminating evidence hidden in his shop.

The first thing he had to do was get rid of it, he decided. All of it. He would have enough money to buy another stash anyway. He could not take any chances, but not before having a few snorts of blow first. It would give him just the jump-start he needed to get his butt in gear. Life was starting to look good.

Chapter 21: Insightful Instincts

"Terrance!"

"Hi, Jacqueline."

"You startled me. I didn't realize that was you behind me."

Her heart hiccupped upon seeing him. She wondered—could he have been the person that was following her? Though she never had a reason to fear him before, she started doubting herself. Had he been tailgating her earlier?

"How've you been?"

"I'm fine, Terrance, and you?" She hoped her voice was not as shaky as she thought it was.

"Doing well."

He paused, as if he wanted to say something but was expecting Jacqueline to speak.

"What brings you out over here?" Her hands gripped her packages more tightly. Her palms were starting to sweat and her mouth was dry, as if she had swallowed a layer of sandpaper and washed it down with baking soda.

"Just going shopping. I saw you get out of your car and I didn't want to scare you, so I figured I'd wait until you were finished."

"Wow, I've been here for almost an hour. You waited that long?" The tiny hairs on her neck stood straight up, and she realized she was tense.

"Well, now that you say it like that, I sound like a stalker." His smile reassured her that he was one of the good guys, but she still had some doubt.

"No, I went and got a coffee down at the other end of the shopping center and came back. By that time, you were already on line. Hope I didn't freak you out at all."

She wanted to scream, "Yes! You did. Stop it. I can't take any more this week," but she refrained and instead answered more politely. "No, it's just been a tough week. Strange things have happened, unfortunate things. I'm a little on edge."

"Yeah, I read about it in the newspaper. That's kinda why I waited for you. I wanted to make sure that you were okay." She lifted her head to meet his eyes. "I'm sorry to hear about that. I'm sure that wasn't easy on you."

"Well, no. It's not, and thank you. I didn't even realize it had hit the papers. I guess it makes sense that it would've." She began to feel a little more at ease. He wasn't threatening her. He wasn't asking her for anything. He was just talking like a normal human being—something that she didn't feel like at the moment. Instead, she felt more like an alien whose ship had landed at the wrong place at the wrong time.

"Well, it was good seeing you, Jackie. I hope things get better for you. I gotta run. Literally. I'm participating in a marathon tomorrow and gotta get some rest. Take care."

"You too, Terrance. It was nice to see you, and good luck in the marathon!" She was relieved that he was over her, and taken aback that he was no longer clingy.

They hugged good-bye, and she watched as he got into his truck.

She shook her head and chuckled. *He drives a truck. It wasn't him following me earlier. That psycho following me was driving a car. Now it is official. I think everyone is out to get me and I have completely lost my freaking mind.*

When she got back in her car, hot tears streamed down her face. *I'm going crazy. Terrance? How could I honestly think that he would be terrorizing me? He was never abusive. Not once did he lay a hand on me. Come to think of it, he never even cursed at me. Why the heck am I so relentlessly on edge?*

Her dim thoughts were interrupted by the annoying ring of her cell phone.

"Jacqueline?"

"Yeah, hi Ben."

"Hey, are you home?"

"Um, heading home now. What's up?"

"Well, nothing to be worried about, but I just saw a white car park in front of your house."

"What?!"

"Don't get alarmed. I wouldn't have called, but the person walked in your backyard. I didn't know if you were expecting anyone."

"Oh my God, no. I wasn't. Is he still there?"

"No, he just left. I saw him walk out from your yard and go outside, but he got in his car and drove off before I could reach him."

A host of different scenarios clogged her imagination like a backed-up sink. "I'm coming home."

"Okay, and Jacqueline?"

"Yes?"

"It looked like he was carrying something. It seemed like it was a black pole—did you have anything like that in your yard?"

She remembered her supposed hallucination from the other night, of the man walking through her yard carrying what she had thought was a pole.

She was not losing her mind, though now she sort of wished that she was. Someone had been there, after all.

Chapter 22: Misguided

When she rushed up her driveway, Ben looked like he half-expected her car to coast in on two wheels. He met her and opened her car door. "Whoa! Speed demon. Slow down. Are you okay?"

Not much in the mood for small talk, Jacqueline surveyed her property before even saying hello. "Well, okay I guess, except for this mystery person trespassing on my property. Were you able to get a good look? Was it a guy or a girl?"

"I'm pretty certain it was a guy. Looked that way. By the time I noticed and came outside, they were already in the car."

"They? As in more than one?"

"No, no. There was just one person."

"Okay, so let me get this straight: he went into the yard, brought out a black pole, and drove away?"

"Listen, as far as I can tell, that's all I saw. I'm not sure how long he was there. It couldn't be too long because I only got home about an hour ago and the car wasn't there then."

"This is all wrong." Jacqueline looked away and shook her head. "Something is going on."

"What do you mean?"

"Well, last night after I caused such a ruckus, I looked outside of the kitchen window and Ben, I swear to you, I thought I saw a man—or woman—or a weird nomadic rhinoceros for that matter, walking in my backyard with a black pole." She shook her head, disappointed with herself for not trusting her gut instinct. "When I got a better look, all I could see in the darkness were trees and rainfall and not much else. I brushed it off and figured I was being ridiculous, but now…" Her voice trailed off as she tried to collect her thoughts.

"So, someone was there. Aside from you imagining the alarm going off, there really was a person on your property. He probably dropped the pole and went back today to get it."

"Yeah. The scary thing about that is what if I was home today? Would he have broken in? And, what in the world was he doing with a pole? As far as I know, I didn't have anything like that back there." Ben just nodded. He couldn't think of anything to say, since it seemed he was starting to agree with Jacqueline. "Unless…"

"Unless what?"

"Well, today on my way to the stores, someone was tailgating me. He would not leave me alone. When I pulled into the shopping center, the car veered off, but it was very strange. Then, an hour later, I bumped into Terrance at the department store."

"Wow, all this before noon? You truly do live an exciting life!"

"I guess you can say I've been quite busy making enemies in my spare time."

"So, what do you want to do about it?"

"I don't know. I mean, if I call the cops again, they are going to commit me to the loony bin. Maybe it was my landlord in the backyard. Who knows? To be quite honest, I am sick of being afraid. I wish they would just show themselves if they have some secret vendetta with me. Instead, they sneak around when I am sleeping or follow me on the road? When I'm not looking over my shoulder, I'm spending the rest of my time getting more and more outraged!"

"Amazing. Now you are starting to sound like the logical one."

"Well, this may sound completely bizarre, but believe it or not, I used to be logical once upon a time. I can only deal with so much before I start losing my temper. I don't want to live like this."

"Perhaps we should get the police over here one more time, to check out the property."

"No, let me check inside. I'll know if anyone has been in my house. If all looks okay, I won't call them. I don't want to be crying wolf all the time."

"Jackie, I'm here for you. If you haven't figured it out yet, I care about you a great deal. I know it's silly. We've known each other less than a week, but I can't help but have feelings for you and if it is okay with you, I'd like you to stay alive for a bit."

"Feelings, huh?"

"Yes, do I need to repeat myself?"

"Well, it couldn't hurt."

"Jacqueline, I think I am falling for you."

"Well, Ben, that feeling is mutual." She leaned in for a kiss, but this time it was he who backed off.

"Sorry to ask this, but do you think Terrance would have come here?"

"Impossible. I had just run into him at the shopping center and was speaking to him right about the time that you called." She thought back to what Terrance said about getting a coffee while he waited for her to shop and wondered if he would have made it to her house and back in time. "Did the person *just* leave when you called me?"

"Yep, about a minute before."

"Oh, okay, then no. It couldn't have been Terrance."

"So do you think you'll be okay?"

"Yes, Ben, but you're just across the street. If anything happens, I'll call you. I hope that's all right with you?"

"I wouldn't have it any other way. What are your plans now?"

"I have to go back out. There are still some more errands I have to tend to, including the dentist. I'm wondering if I should reschedule that appointment. At the rate I'm going, they'll probably have some crazed man dressed in a white coat claiming to be a dentist who will find self-gratification in pulling all of my teeth, or something equally painful."

Amused at her attempt to make a small joke, he rolled his eyes. "I think you'll be okay there. If they so much as cause you an ounce of pain, you call me baby, I'll take care of him for ya."

"Ooh, I like the way that sounds."

Ben stayed with her while she searched her house. After she checked each room, she realized not a thing was out of place. "Okay, so I guess I had better go and get things done. If you see anything odd, please let me know."

"Other than a highly-stressed out female driver with crazy stalkers following her? Sure."

"Very funny. Yes, other than that."

"Okay. Hey, dinner tonight at Henry's?"

Henry's Restaurant was a bar and grill located on the water. It was notorious for impressive first dates—and tear-jerking breakups. Jacqueline was fairly certain that Ben wasn't planning on breaking off something that had barely started yet.

"Well, sure, if I still have all of my teeth."

"Okay. If not, I'll ask if they can puree it for you. See you later."

Chapter 23: Stalked

By the time she had finished her errands and had had her fair share of torture at the dentist, Jacqueline was borderline exhausted. She couldn't wait to get home and take a nap before her big date with Ben.

To her astonishment, she wasn't even concerned about the person in her yard, or about any of the events over the course of the past few days. All she truly cared about was catching up on some much-needed sleep. She found her edginess was working in her favor to some degree, as the more this mystery person silently harassed her, the angrier she became. It was not as if the terror had fully disappeared, since she still felt plenty of it, but she was getting ready to fight.

She made a right-hand turn onto Main Street and then turned left onto Galveston Drive. She looked in her rearview mirror and that was the precise moment when she noticed that driving behind her, in a beat-up white sedan, was the same person that had tailgated her earlier that day. This time, there was no one else was on the road, and the two cars were so close that she could not even see the car's front bumper. There were some houses on the street spread acres apart, but for the most part, it was a straightaway that connected two major intersections. Though the speed limit was thirty-five, she sped up and just like she had conceptualized, so did the driver. The person swerved to the left of her as if to pass, but then drove the car in line right behind her, before performing the same maneuver on the right-hand side. There was clearly plenty of room to pass on the left, but the driver didn't. He or she was toying with her and seemed to be enjoying it.

In an instant, Jacqueline felt threatened. She came to the harsh realization that it was not a mild case of paranoia or strange, intermittent hallucinations. It was not stress, and although she hadn't slept much lately, it was not exhaustion.

This was real. The driver exercised more aggression, following and mimicking her every move. They veered sporadically all over the road, coming dangerously close to skimming her bumper and trying to corner her. Where there weren't houses, there were trees, lots of them. She realized it was the driver's goal to cause Jacqueline to crash her car into one of them without causing damage to the driver's own already-beat-up car, and the driver was clever. If their car never touched hers, no one could tie him or her to Jacqueline's accident. The cops may even believe she swerved to avoid hitting a cat. At one point, the driver accelerated up and drove right beside her. They were so close that if she wanted to, she could actually touch the passenger-side door.

She had to keep her eyes on the road, but at the same time, knew it was necessary to call for help. This was too much for her to handle on her own. If there was some remote chance that she could exploit this person and end this once and for all, she needed to take it.

Motivated by fear, she fumbled around on the front seat of her car and in the console in search of her cell phone. She was always misplacing it, and this time she regretted her carelessness. Her first instinct was to call the police, even though she still worried that they would think she was a crazy lady after her false—or maybe not-so-false—alarm the other night. But she dialed the police station anyway and gave them her whereabouts. If nothing else, they might be able to send an ambulance, should the driver cause any bodily harm to her.

Her next rational notion was to call Ben. Though it was possible that he thought of her as a little insane, at least he knew about what had been going on the past few days. With her eyes on the road and her fingers on the keypad, she dialed his number. It rang three times before he answered, and to Jacqueline, it seemed like forever. "Ben?"

"Jacqueline, hey!"

"Ben, he's following me again. He's right behind me in a white car."

"What do you mean? Now? Where?"

"Yes!

"Do you know who it is?"

"No."

"Have you seen his face?"

"No."

"How do you know it is a he?"

"I don't. Could be a she. I thought it was a coincidence. Same car, same nauseous feeling in the pit of my stomach. Ben, he's going to kill me."

"Jackie, what kind of car is it?"

"I have to call you back. If you do not hear from me or if something happens to me, it was against my will. I gotta go. He's driving erratically now. I can't talk!"

"Jacqueline, wait, where are you?" Silence. "Jacqueline? JACQUELINE?!"

Her mind was now racing faster than the revolving wheels on her car. More than ever, she needed to remain as calm as possible and keep her wits about her. The driver of the vehicle was after her with a vengeance. She still had no clue as to why.

She was able to glance again at the person following her. This time he took off his sunglasses. He also took off his hat. She tried to get a good look, but at the same time was fearful of catching eyes with him.

It was a male from what she could tell. His windows were slightly tinted, so she could not get an accurate focus.

He was yelling something to her. Of course, she couldn't hear him, but she did know that he had set out to torment her. He had tracked her every move. She was the focal point of his attention. She wondered how she ever became so lucky.

There was only a mile or two to go before she would encounter an intersection. Surely there would be more cars on the road, and she stood a greater chance at losing him or at least sharing the road with witnesses. Chances are if people were around, he would stop—she hoped.

She sped up, not so worried this time about getting a speeding ticket, and as she suspected he would, the driver flew up along with her and kept the pace. As they each approached the intersection, his hands were waving in the air and he pulled an imaginary trigger. Within seconds, he bolted in front of her and without stopping, made a right-hand turn on the busy intersection, without even looking to check if it was clear. He was gone before she could read the make and model of the car. She couldn't even get his license plate number, if he had one.

Though she was a firm believer in karma, she couldn't help but hope for the worst for her new stalker. In her heart of hearts, she only wished someone would run him off of the road and slam *his* car into a tree. If not, he was free to stalk her another day, and for the first time in years, she couldn't pretend to be brave anymore; she was truly terrified.

Chapter 24: Momentum

As Jacqueline lost sight of her stalker, she did her very best to gain her composure. The pressure on her chest felt as if it were prohibiting her from breathing until she realized she had forgotten to.

As she sucked in the humid air, she felt a kick of life reborn. *I am still alive. He may be some sick bastard, but he did not win this time. I am definitely alive. For now.*

It occurred to Jacqueline that although her feelings of paranoia had been magnified these past couple of days, this situation was very real. She couldn't have imagined that the same driver from earlier that day was stalking her.

But what in the world did he want? Aside from minor mishaps out of her control, she had never made any enemies. She didn't have a naturally mean bone in her body. She was not evil, like some of those people she'd read about in the paper or on the Internet.

She'd sometimes hear about rivals getting revenge on each other, or a husband finding his wife sleeping with another man and thinking he has the right to create his own justice. Or teenagers pulling a gun on each other just to show who's boss. It was pointless.

But Jacqueline had never been like that; she kept to herself. She didn't cause trouble and certainly never went out to find it. Was this random? Did some strange guy that she had never met before have a secret vendetta against her? Could it possibly be a coincidence that this same driver found her twice in one day and it was his goal in life to scare the wits out of a lone girl?

Whatever the reasoning, she knew she was going to see him again. There was no doubt in her mind, and she had to come up with a game plan for the next time it happened.

What could she possibly do to save her own life? She would have liked to have started with recording his license plate, but from what she could tell, there wasn't one for her to record, and she had been horrified to note the make and model of the car.

She called the police and let them know that the driver had sped away. She offered his description, as lame as it was. Except for the fact that he wore a black cap and sunglasses, she had nothing else to go on. She couldn't even tell his hair or eye color. The only thing she was somewhat sure of at this point was that it *was* a *he,* although even that wasn't definite.

She needed a plan. If she was going to put an end to this harassment, she needed to brainstorm. This could quite conceivably be a matter of life or death. She preferred that it wasn't the latter.

Her knuckles were white as she gripped the steering wheel and headed for home, wildly looking in every direction for any sign of a threat. Her mind displayed dismal images of what might happen next. It was as if she had her own private screening to a movie made solely for her. She envisioned his car bursting out from the trees on the side of the road, or waiting for her in her garage.

In some instances, having an overactive imagination is more of a curse than a blessing. This was one of those instances.

From all of the articles she had read about stress, it was more often than not self-inflicted.

She tried to erase the horrific feeling of alarm and replace it with rationalization. Unfortunately, she was failing miserably. Not one rational thought drifted through her mind.

The person driving that car had a purpose. Now, Jacqueline needed one too. An assortment of ideas swirled in her mind like an eerie rainbow of colors. Would she need a guard dog? How about a large knife? Where would she put it, under her pillow? She pictured herself fortuitously slicing her own hands on its jagged edge, blood dripping onto her pillow while her stalker sat back and laughed.

The thought of buying a gun briefly entered her mind. It was something she didn't truly want to consider, since the idea of actually using one made her uneasy, and plus, she had a black belt in tae kwon do. Her hands could be considered a lethal weapon. Why would she need a gun?

She recalled a family acquaintance talking about how he shot an intruder in the stomach, though it turned out to be a friend that came over in an effort to surprise him. Would Jacqueline make that same awful mistake if she bought a gun? She envisioned herself shooting her father in the middle of the night.

No, for her a gun just wouldn't work. Her nerves were already rattled; she would be trigger-happy at the slightest stray noise.

All of these things started happening when she moved into her new house. Come to think of it, it all happened when she first met Ben. Could this be his doing?

She then thought back to the night of the accident with Shelby. Was she destined to be tortured from that point on? Was this all the proof she needed that karma did exist? Was it her turn to pay the piper...again?

Maybe Detective Brown was after her. Did he not believe her after all? Perhaps there was a reason he was seeking revenge. Was he close with Shelby, maybe a relative?

She thought back to Terrance and how she briefly believed he was following her. Who would so such a thing?

Driving at speeds that would easily get her arrested, her mind raced with horrifying thoughts. She found herself talking to herself more than usual. *Just get home, Jacqueline. Park the car in the garage. Go to sleep.*

She pulled into her driveway seconds later and everything seemed as it should be, though she couldn't help but scrutinize her surroundings as she pulled in. Anything was possible and she was on high alert.

Ben ran out of his house as he watched her pull up. She felt a mountain of guilt as she saw him approach. He had been nothing but kind and decent to her. How could she think such thoughts about him? He would never be responsible for torturing her, not in a million years.

She had barely stopped the car when Ben opened her door. "Hey, are you okay?" he asked.

"I think so."

She got out and he wrapped his arms around her. She was shivering, even though the temperature was in the mid-seventies.

"It was so very odd, Ben. I thought for sure he was going to kill me. He would not let up. I think he had followed me for a full twenty minutes before cutting me off and fleeing away. Truthfully, I don't know why he didn't finish me off right then and there. Why he is torturing me, I'll never know!"

"So, it was a man? Did you get a good look?"

"It was a man. I'm pretty sure. I got a brief look, but I couldn't tell you what he looked like. He didn't stay in my vision long enough once he took off his sunglasses. He drove off like a bat out of hell once I was even able to focus."

"Okay, Jackie, this is getting out of hand. Maybe we should get the cops here."

"No, no. I already called them and then called them back to say I was okay. They are going to think I am some fanatical woman with too much time on her hands who enjoys crying wolf every ten minutes."

"Let's just call them. You do what you can and tell them what you know. At least there will be a report filed. So what if they think you are crazy?"

The thought of summoning the police to her house one more time left her with a twisted feeling in the pit of her stomach. She felt like she was starting to recognize the 911 operator's voice, as well as a good portion of the police force.

Ben was staring at her with his cell phone in his hand, waiting to get Jacqueline's blessing.

"I'm sorry. I can't do it, Ben. They have the telephone report. That should be good enough for now. I feel like a psychotic lunatic. I couldn't even give a description of the car. All I know is that it was a beat-up white sedan. That's all I got. I have no idea where this guy is, what he looks like, or what he would want with me. As of days ago, I didn't have any enemies, at least none that I knew of." Ben nodded. "Let's just leave it for now. I've had enough excitement for one day. As a matter of fact, I've had enough excitement for a whole year. I want my mundane life back. No police officers, no psycho chasing me all over town."

"I get it."

"I'd love to believe that he wanted to get his thrills and frighten me. Some sick teen on a joyride or dare. Mission accomplished. Perhaps now he'll leave me alone."

"Perhaps. For all you know, he might be torturing some other helpless girl. Or perhaps he'll come back here for more. Is that something you can deal with?"

Before answering, she considered her options.

"I'll have to. I have no choice."

Chapter 25: Identity Confirmed

A loud rap at the door woke Donovan from a hazy state of unconsciousness. "One minute!" Mumbling to himself, he scrambled across the room, looking for a pair of shorts and a T-shirt. Opening the door, he didn't look up before speaking. "What the hell do you want?"

"Are you Donovan Murray?" Two police officers greeted him at the door.

"Yes. Do you realize it is six o'clock in the freaking morning?"

"I apologize sir, but this couldn't wait. We believe something has happened to your partner."

"My partner? I don't have a partner."

"Your business partner, sir."

"I don't have a business partner. Do your damn research. We dissolved the business. I'm going solo until all of our affairs are in order. I assume you are talking about Carmine?"

"Yes."

"Well, speak! What about him?"

"Easy there, sir. Like I said, we believe something happened to him."

"Fantastic. Like what? Would you get to the point already?"

"We believe he might have been murdered."

"Nah, Carmine? He could take care of himself. Murdered? Never."

"Sir, we found a body in the bay south of Main Street."

"It's not Carmine's. I just saw him last week."

"We need you to identify the body. He had his wallet on him. No next of kin was listed."

"Yeah, he doesn't talk to his family." He realized he had spoken about him in the present tense, and then figured that probably worked to his benefit. "Carmine is heavily into drugs and his family disowned him years ago."

"Well, he listed you as his ICE."

"His what?"

"In case of emergency. His ICE."

"You guys have fancy acronyms for everything these days, don't ya?" The two officers rolled their eyes and nodded. Once he realized they were not going to leave without him, he gave in. "Okay. Hang on and let me get dressed. It's cold out there. I'm telling you though, it ain't him."

Chapter 26: Moment of Truth

As they peeled back the blanket to show him Carmine's remains, a tidal wave of nausea rolled through Donovan's stomach. He certainly didn't expect to feel anything this powerful.

He wasn't stupid. He already knew Montgomery was to blame for this. Donovan had had no part of it. What he was guilty of was buying large quantities of drugs and hiding the stash in his shop. Lastly, he had an even bigger role in hiding those same drugs in Carmine's house.

He started to feel some guilt over planting the drugs there, but in truth, Carmine was already dead. Nothing else could hurt him now. It wasn't like he had a reputation to uphold or if he did, that anyone would be surprised. He was a drug addict.

The cops were bound to search his house for evidence. Carmine's fingerprints had already been all over the stash. The cops would then put their clues together, realizing that his murder was a drug deal gone awry. This was the insurance that Donovan needed to keep his name clean. Hell, if Carmine was alive, he wouldn't hate Donovan for it. He of all people would understand.

When he got himself together, Donovan nodded his head and pursed his lips. After a moment, he mumbled, "That's him."

The two officers looked at each other, and the taller of the two spoke first. "Do you mind answering a few questions for us? Just some routine stuff, but we need to know where to look first."

"Sure, officer. I can do that."

The officers brought in their detectives, and they began to question him. They delved into their history, how

Donovan and Carmine first met, and when they started the business together. Like he knew they would, the detectives asked about Carmine's habits—people he knew and hung out with, what he did after work. They also inquired about other employees and, since he was on the payroll, Donovan had to reveal Montgomery as an ex-employee, although he didn't divulge why they had let him go. If needed, he would lie and blame it on the termination of the business, rather than the real reason—burglary.

After a relatively painless series of questions, they let Donovan go without naming him as a suspect. They did, however, explain to him that he was a person of interest, until further notice.

Their next stop was the home of Montgomery Vendora. They only hoped he would be just as cooperative.

Chapter 27: Standard Procedure

When they arrived at his home, Montgomery appeared aloof and confident.

The officers explained the reason for their visit to his apartment. Montgomery seemed all too happy to join them at the station for questioning.

Once they arrived at the station, Detective Brown took charge of the questioning while the two officers observed. He discovered that Carmine was with Montgomery the day of the murder. Montgomery explained that they had two jobs to do that day and that Carmine had complained of a severe back ache, so he sat in the van for most of the work while Montgomery handled the majority of it on his own.

He gave details about how installing a water heater was usually a two-man job, but that he had been able to handle it by himself. He bragged about this, as if the detective was supposed to be impressed by his incredible strength.

Montgomery's right leg involuntarily shook up and down while he was speaking, and he alternated between chewing on the tips of his fingers and twisting his bottom lip between his thumb and forefinger.

Detective Brown commented that it looked like he was devouring a juicy steak. "Montgomery, are you on drugs?"

"Nope."

"Are ya sure? You seem a little fidgety."

"No drugs, sir."

"Okay, do think you can keep your fingers out of your mouth for a while? We're having some difficulty understanding you."

A darkening glare dimmed Montgomery's eyes. The detective had gotten to him, and he didn't like to be challenged. He felt he was above that. No, Montgomery was a smug son-of-a-bitch. He wasn't going down without a fight.

"Were you and Carmine close?" The detective continued his questioning without skipping a beat or acknowledging the uncomfortable shift in Montgomery's posture, though he sure as hell noticed it.

"Nah, we partied together and we worked together. Hell, we partied while we worked." He laughed about it, like he was expecting the task force to laugh with him. "That's about it. Carmine would party all day if he had the chance. That guy was something else. Hell, I never saw anyone do the half the shit that Carmine did. Damn legend if you ask me."

"I thought a minute ago you just said you weren't on drugs."

"I'm not on drugs *now*. But yeah, I do drugs every now and then, you know, socially."

"Uh-huh. How much drugs do you do?"

The legs started shaking a bit more now and Montgomery shrugged, his confidence dwindling just a little. "Not that much. Everybody does them now and then. I'm not addicted or anything stupid like that. What's the big deal?"

The detective continued. "Did you and Carmine ever fight? Have a disagreement? Become violent?"

"Nope." Montgomery looked to his left at a picture on the wall.

"You know, Montgomery, they say when people lie, they often look up and to the left."

"So?" His focus was now straight in front of him, but he still didn't look the detective in the eye.

"It's an interesting fact, isn't it?"

"I guess so."

"Do you like that picture on the wall?"

"It's okay."

"You were just looking there."

"I'm bored."

"An innocent man has been murdered and you're bored?"

"Are you accusing me of a crime or not?"

"I can if you'd like me to. Did you have anything to do with it?"

"I had nothing to do with his death. Have you ever met him? Always looked like he was sucking on sour grapes. He was a junkie, man. Anyone could have gotten to him. I'm sure he made enemies wherever he went."

"Possibly, however; he was with you that day."

"No, only during the day. I never hung out with that loser after hours."

"Montgomery, we are still investigating the specifics of this case, but we are going to need you to stay in town for the next couple of days. Think you can manage that for us?"

"Sure, I guess so." He paused long enough to smirk. "I *was* supposed to go on a trip to England to visit the queen, but I suppose that I'll have to tell her our plans have been canceled. She's going to be mad at me. She's going to be even more infuriated with you since you are the one that made me miss our date. You know what they say—you don't want to keep the queen waiting."

Ignoring his snide remarks and facetious attitude, Detective Brown dismissed him. "Thank you for your time, Mr. Vendora. Please stay in this state."

"Oh, we are all done already?"

Without looking up from his memo pad, the detective answered him. "For now."

"Great, which is the way out?"

"Officer Shore will take you there."

Once they dismissed him, the officers all reconvened in a circle to discuss any leads. Their forensics team had been searching for evidence at the shop that Carmine shared with Donovan, as well as Carmine's house. The last place they searched was in the videotapes at the shop. Donovan had tried to hide them, but they found them in a drawer. Donovan claimed that Carmine must have watched them, because he had never seen them. He hoped they believed his little white lie. He had also parked the work van at another location, fearing that they might find evidence in there. Surprisingly, Montgomery had done a hell of a job cleaning whatever blood might have leaked out, but the van smelled of death, at least to Donovan. He had conflicted emotions on whether he should leave the van as is, or clean it up more. He wanted them to find Montgomery guilty, but only once any incriminating evidence against Donovan himself was destroyed.

"What did you find?" Brown asked Officer Stoddard.

"Montgomery stole from them. Clear as day on this videotape."

"Stole from Donovan and Carmine?"

"Yes."

"Well, isn't that something?"

"Donovan said he never saw the tape?"

"That's what he said."

"Really? Why is that?"

"I dunno. He said Carmine always handled that. Maybe Carmine saw them and didn't get a chance to tell Donovan. Maybe the killer got to Carmine before he got to them."

Brown rubbed his chin. "Interesting. So it looks like Montgomery might've wanted Carmine to keep quiet, huh?" Not waiting for an answer, he looked toward the window as if he wanted confirmation from outside. He nodded slowly. "Good job, Stoddard." Just when it seemed that the detective was holding it all together, he pounded his fists down on the desk. "Dammit! Did I just let our prime suspect walk? Stoddard, call for backup and go to this address. We need to apprehend him immediately. He could very well be the prime and only suspect in this case. We need him back here. I want DNA samples, fingerprints, the works. Is that clear?"

"Yes, sir! I'm on it."

"Williams?"

"Yes?"

"Get a composite sketch of this guy just in case. Call Donovan and see if he has any photographs of Montgomery. If he's guilty, he could be out of the country in a few hours."

"You got it."

The officers scurried around the station before they left on their respective duties. Detective Brown paced the floor like an expectant father as he waited to hear back from his team.

Hours passed and they kept in constant contact. But by sundown, they still hadn't found him.

"That son of a bitch! He's skipped town. I can feel it."

Officer Williams reported back first. "Donovan had no pictures, sir. I'm sorry."

"It's okay. We have a pretty lifelike sketch."

The room was silent. Everyone felt it. They knew they had their guy, in theory. They just did not have him in custody and they didn't have a clue as to where he was.

"Tammy, call Channel Seven. We need to get this on the air now."

"Detective, are you sure?"

"I'm taking the risk; I'll take the blame. I want his picture out there. If he's innocent, he'll waltz right back in here…but I'll be damned if he's not guilty as sin."

Chapter 28: Rain Check?

"Ben, please don't take offense, but I really just want to be alone tonight. Can we skip our date and take a rain check?"

With his hand on his heart, he sunk to his knees and gave an Academy Award-winning performance. "Oh, that hurt. I've been rejected." She smirked at his acting and helped him off of the floor. "Seriously, Jackie, are you sure? Maybe getting your mind off of this freak of nature is what you need."

"Yeah, probably, but the truth is that I'm exhausted, anxious, and I just want to go to sleep. I desperately need to get some rest and wrap my mind around the troubles of this past week. I'm hoping to wake up and find that it all is a nasty dream."

"You mean nightmare."

"Yes, definitely a nightmare!"

"Okay, go relax and get some sleep. I'll leave my phone right by my nightstand. If you need me, just call me or come in. Here's my key. No need to knock. Just walk in and wake me." He reached down into his front pants pocket and pulled out a small keychain with a single key on it.

Grabbing his key, she sighed. "Ya know, I have to admit something to you that I am not proud of."

"Uh-oh. That's never good."

"No, I'm ashamed, but I feel like I need to get this off of my chest."

"Okay, what is it?"

"In an indirect kind of way, I blamed you for this while I was driving."

"Me?!"

"I'm sorry! I just was trying to piece this all together and while I was driving, I calculated that the drama started happening once I met you. I'm sorry. I'm being silly. I know that. You, of all people, have been nothing short of wonderful to me."

"Oh, this takes the cake. I've been rejected and insulted!" He nudged her with his shoulder to show that he was teasing and not in the least bit insulted. The last thing she needed right now was a guilt trip. "I'm not a stalker. I don't hurt women…or men for that matter, unless they hurt my woman!"

His imitation of a body builder left much to be desired, but he achieved his goal of putting a smile on Jacqueline's face. She chuckled. "Thank you for that. I definitely need some comic relief. I'll see you tomorrow, okay? Don't hate me. I have to get myself together or at least give it an honest attempt."

"Don't worry about it. I respect your decision. I may not agree with it, but I respect it. Okay, tomorrow it is. I'm holding you to it."

"I promise—it's a plan. I have work in the morning of course, but after that, dinner."

"Okay, get some sleep. Don't want no haggard-looking ol' lady accompanying me on my hot date tomorrow evening."

"Thanks a lot!"

"Just kidding. May I at least steal a kiss good-night or do I have to beg?"

"Well, a little begging would be nice at this point, but I guess I won't make you go through all of that. After all, you have been a good sport."

After they said good-bye, Jacqueline threw on a pair of shorts and a tank top, locked her windows and doors, and set the security alarm, this time making sure that the light was a solid red.

Once she slid under the covers, her body sunk lazily into the mattress, enabling sleep to embrace her with open arms.

Chapter 29: Exposed!

On the other side of town, in a quiet, smoky pub, Montgomery sipped his draft beer, confident that he had evaded punishment once again.

After the bartender poured Montgomery another brew, he excused himself to tend to another patron. At that same moment, a bad sitcom was blaring from the television that hung from the ceiling over the bar. The program was interrupted by a reporter getting ready to give a breaking news report.

"Police are on the lookout for this individual. His name is Montgomery Vendora. He is a possible suspect in the murder of Carmine Stuckey, whose body was found in the bay late yesterday afternoon. Police believe there might have been an argument over stolen goods from a company where Vendora was once employed. He is to be considered armed and very dangerous. If you know this man or think that you know this man, please dial the number located at the bottom of your television screen. All calls will remain anonymous and be kept confidential. Please do not under any circumstances make an attempt to apprehend this man yourself. He was last seen driving a white sedan with the license plate number shown below."

On the television screen was a sketched image that easily resembled Montgomery. As he looked up at the screen and recognized his own face, he looked around the quiet bar and downed his beer. Lucky for him, he was surrounded by self-absorbed, well-inebriated patrons, so no one seemed to make the connection.

When he had the chance, he quietly slipped out of the bar, got into his car, and sped away. He reached into his glove box for a screwdriver and raced to a parking lot, where he was able to switch the license plates on his car with another.

Overwhelmed, he had to pull into a safe haven where he could collect his thoughts and devise a game plan. He couldn't go to his house. For sure the cops would be waiting for him.

He wondered if the police had any other evidence on him, other than the video of him stealing tools. If not, they certainly couldn't incriminate him on those petty charges alone. If he felt like they could, he would be more apt to skip town, but he was cocky enough to stay and make them prove his guilt.

He almost laughed to himself at the detectives' foolishness, but then he reminded himself about Jacqueline. He had meant to do away with her from the moment she noticed the blood in the van. She could quite feasibly be the key witness for the police department and their case against him. The day he had followed her to the beach, he thought he might have some quality time with her, but there had been too many people. He had tried to break into her house, but she must have heard something to wake her. It bothered him that he couldn't figure out how she knew he was there. Even today when he had followed her in the car, it wasn't safe. He couldn't have taken the chance. If only she would have pulled over out of fear or imprudence, he might have been able to finish the job with one bullet.

Tonight had to be the night. Jacqueline had two strikes against her as far as he was concerned. He wasn't going to give her the opportunity to get to three.

She was responsible for killing his girlfriend, Shelby, claiming it was an *accident*. He didn't believe it for one moment. Sure, Shelby had done a little more heroin than usual that night, but she would never pass out in the middle of the street like that. Montgomery had little doubt that Jacqueline fabricated that part of the story.

If that wasn't bad enough, she was also the one missing link that could sentence him to a lifetime behind bars. She knew that Montgomery had been working alone the day he installed the water-heater. She was aware that no one else had been in that van—alive, anyway. Most importantly, she had seen the blood. She knew him from a previous lifetime and was more than familiar with his questionable history. She would be the one to assist the cops. It was only a matter of days before she realized he had been the one at her house that day. They would make it a point to speak to her and get her statement.

Yes, tonight was the night. Sweet Jacqueline could kiss her terrified ass good-bye.

Chapter 30: Beware!

As Jacqueline drifted into a peaceful sleep, her mind floated effortlessly to another time—one where she was safe and free from the drug scene, from car chases and stalkers, and from the stresses of the day.

Her body floated as if she were on a cotton-filled cloud, soaring through the sky. In this weightless world, her body was at rest. Her mind was clear. She felt revived.

The warming sun sheltered her as she relaxed in her backyard. It was late afternoon and the rays were still bright. The steady hum of the filter from the built-in pool delivered a wonderful white noise, blocking out any of the sounds of traffic coming from the street. Though not quite ready for a swim, she dipped her toes in the pool and sat on the ledge. The tepid water was cerulean blue and crystal-clear. She could see all the way down to the bottom.

From the corner of her eye, she saw something move in the bushes and scurry across the yard. When he got closer, she recognized him instantly. His beautiful golden coat glistened in the summer sun and his soulful eyes were ones that she could never forget. He had a gentle demeanor; all seemed right with the world whenever he appeared. She just never knew when that time would come. Though he was still a young dog, his communicative eyes were that of an old soul, filled with loyalty, caring, concern, and love.

She had only seen him a few times before today. The last time had been in the park. From what she recalled, his name was Butter. He wore it proudly on a tan, peanut-shaped tag that hung around his neck. The tag even resembled an actual peanut, with the ridges and indentations to go along with it. Though she had never seen a dog tag of that shape, she found it fitting for him.

He walked, a beautiful grin across his face, carrying what appeared to be a sock in his mouth, with his tennis ball attached to his collar around his neck.

"Butter! Hi there. You came back!"

He wagged his fluffy tail at the sound of her voice and nudged her hand with his muzzle, dropping the sock in her lap. She gave him a big hug as he approached and kissed the top of his nose. His blond fur was warm to the touch, so she dipped her hand in the pool to cup some water for him, assuming he must be thirsty. He drank gently from her hand, watching her face the entire time. Once he was done, she sprinkled a little water on him to cool him off. At first he seemed to enjoy it, biting the water as it splashed toward him. A look of laughter was painted on his face as he snuggled next to Jacqueline.

After a brief moment, he slowly backed away and crouched down, barking at her with a stern look of worry expressed in his eyes. Again, he barked with caution and backed up.

"Butter! It's just water, sweetie. It's nothing to worry about. It won't hurt you."

He barked and growled some more before crawling over to her, lightly grabbing her hand and gripping it in his mouth.

"All right, Butter. Let me just go in real quick to cool off and then I'll come with you, I promise. You can show me what is bothering you, okay?"

Her slender calves had barely touched the water when Butter's bark elevated into more of a ferocious growl. His sudden fear of the pool startled Jacqueline and she tried her best to understand what was causing his distress.

Though still fearful, the dog made his way over to Jacqueline and tightly grabbed the bottom of her shorts.

"Butter! Stop that!"

He only tightened his grip and pulled, ignoring her pleas. Each tug threw Jacqueline off balance, but also brought her closer to the edge of the pool. Soon, she'd have no choice but to step out of the wading area.

"Butter, enough! You're ripping my shorts!"

He was serious now. Again, he paid no mind to her commands and grabbed her hand as she tried to release his grip on the shorts. Though still not inflicting any pain, he tightened his grip onto her hand and did not let go. She was left with no other choice but to follow his lead.

Only once she was completely out of the water did he calm down and release her hand, licking her fingertips as he did so.

"Butter, what has gotten into you, pal? You're a golden retriever. I thought that you are supposed to love swimming in the water!" As she inched closer to him, water began sprouting from the corners of the pool.

Moments later, the cement began to crack and water forced itself through, spraying upward in consecutive bursts, only it was no longer crystal-clear. Instead, it had turned a blackened color that was, without a doubt, blood. Before long, her entire backyard was covered in a thick layer.

The skies turned gray, and the clouds blocked any traces of the bright sun that had provided warmth only moments prior.

Butter desperately grabbed her hand again and pulled her toward him, beginning to run with her closely by his side. Jacqueline did what she could to keep up the pace. He led her to a safe zone and once the pool and the backyard were no longer in sight, Butter jumped in her lap and once again, smothered her with puppy kisses in what could only be described as appreciation. He seemed to be thanking her for following him.

She cupped his snout in her hands and hugged him close to her body. With one more kiss, he nuzzled against her and then turned away with his head held high, wagging his tail and displaying regal pride.

"Butter, wait! Where are you going?"

As he ran off, she watched once again, looking toward the direction from which he was running. It was apparent he did not want her to follow this time.

Waiting for him was a pack of dogs and cats, wagging their tails and playfully jumping on him as he approached. The skies immediately turned bright blue again as the sun broke through the darkness, directly above him. As usual, he paused to give her one final glance before he and the pack disappeared.

Knowing that he would not return, Jacqueline headed back to view the disaster in her backyard. Not realizing what was happening, she stopped just in time. Within mere seconds, the pool imploded, causing blocks of cement to fall heavily on top of one another. The raft floating in the center of the pool, which Jacqueline had planned on lounging on, became suctioned into a whirlpool before disappearing along with the pool.

She screamed so loudly that she woke herself up and jerked herself up from the mattress. Her body and sheets were drenched in a bath of sweat. Once she was able to take a breath, the first thing she could think of was the dog, and then the pool.

Parched from screaming, she slipped out of bed and dragged her feet onto the plush carpet and into the kitchen, turned on the light, and poured herself a glass of water from the tap.

Still enthralled from the authenticity of the dream, she gazed through her kitchen window and out into the depths of her backyard. "What the...?" Blinking, she looked out toward the pool. She turned on the outside light and got a better look. "Oh my god!"

She dropped the glass into the sink and heard it shatter into a million pieces as she ran outside. She had been trained in this exact type of situation and had to do what she could to help. Timing was everything.

Lying face down in the center of her pool was a person—one that she hoped was still alive.

Chapter 31: Arctic Blast

Without hesitation, Jacqueline fled out of her house through the sliding glass door into her backyard, and jumped into the frigid water. The ice-cold water felt like tiny daggers stabbing her flesh and though the warmer months were approaching, it was still easily forty-five degrees outside this early in the morning. Not only did she need to concern herself with the drowning victim, but hypothermia as well.

It did not even occur to her how this person ended up in her pool or that he might already be dead. She had been a lifeguard for five years, and instinct took over to save a life.

One of the first things she had learned was to remain calm and focused. If she panicked even a little, she could easily put herself, as well as the victim, at risk. Though she was not even sure if the person could hear her, she spoke to him. "I'm here to help you. I don't know if you can hear me, but you're going to be okay." Her voice quivered as she spoke and she only hoped she was telling the truth. In reality, she had no idea if he was going to be okay.

She was usually able to move swiftly through the water, but the coldness was slowing her down considerably. She knew that she had to act fast.

The person was completely immobile. She reached the floating body and grabbed hold of him, doing her best to turn him upwards to get his mouth and nose out of the water, without causing him to choke. For sure, it was a balancing act. She felt that his body, while cold, was not yet rigid. This was a good sign and she was able to breathe a small sigh of relief.

Once she caught her own breath, she looked at the person's face before dragging him to the edge of the pool.

To her surprise, his eyes were wide open, staring directly into hers.

A scream lodged in the bottom of her throat. To her horror, it was a face she recognized all too well: Montgomery Vendora.

His eyes blinked and he smiled. His voice quivered as he spoke. "Thank you, Jacqueline. I didn't know you cared." His enormous hands wrapped around her throat, cutting off her air supply. Screaming was now definitely out of the question. She couldn't fathom what was happening. Was she still in the dream? Where was the golden retriever? No, this was reality. She was living her own private nightmare. "I bet you're wondering why, huh, Jacqueline? Poor, poor Jacqueline. The innocent victim." His hands gripped her throat tighter, cutting off her air. Her body shivered in the water and if she couldn't escape his grasp, it was only a matter of time before she passed out. From what she could tell, he was shivering too. Desperate people do desperate things and at this point, she would do anything. She did not want to die. She didn't know why he was here trying to kill her, but she did know she wanted to live. "This is just perfect isn't it? Not my original plan, but I fell in your pool, slipped right on the damn concrete, but you came out only a moment later to save me. How nice!" She struggled against his hold. They were both shivering. She was sure she wouldn't feel her legs but was relieved once she wiggled them. "You killed Shelby on purpose, huh? Did you know she was my girlfriend? You also saw Carmine's blood in the van, didn't you? You saw the trace of evidence that could bring me down. You're going to have to die, Jackie. Just like Shelby died. I'm sorry. It's cold. I have to get this over with."

The words stung almost more painfully than the water. She wasn't crazy, after all. He *had been* at her house and that *had been* him in the yard carrying that pole. He must have dropped it when the police got there and had had the audacity to go back and retrieve it the next day in broad daylight.

While her first instinct was always to save someone's life, it ran parallel with her first impulse, which was to save her own. She tried to scream again, but as she opened her mouth, he pushed her face into the water. She was certain his intent was to drown her there, but she fought like a demon to not let him win. With every feeble ounce of strength that she had left, she positioned herself on the slippery surface of the pool floor and used the buoyancy to her advantage. With her right leg, she swept Montgomery's leg out from underneath him and forced him to loosen his grip on her throat. In the three seconds that she had to play with, she maneuvered herself to get behind him. He put up a fierce struggle, but what he had in strength, she had in agility. He was bigger than her, but with all of the drugs and alcohol streaming through his body, he was in no way faster.

Her health was top notch, while his was faltering. She had years of training in both swimming and tae kwon do. Now was her chance to use both for her benefit.

Remain calm, Jacqueline. You can do this. You HAVE to do this.

Once she got in the exact position she needed, which was in back of him, she wrapped her left hand around his neck in a V-formation and grasped her other bicep. With her free hand, she pushed the back of his head and applied as much pressure as she could to the back of his neck. She felt his Adam's apple in the center of her arm. He thrashed about and tried twisting his body to release her hold. To her benefit, his legs slipped out from underneath him as she applied more pressure. Her own legs swayed to the side, fear and cold causing her to test her balance. The water proved to be a challenge, as she knew it would. But after a frightening struggle, she felt his body go limp and she had accomplished what she had set out to do—place him in sleeper hold until she could call for assistance.

She tried to catch her breath as she dragged his lifeless body to the edge of the pool, gripping his soaking shirt to pull him out. Though the buoyancy of the water made his body a little lighter, she still exerted all of her energy to lift him onto the concrete.

Once she knew for sure that he was out for the count, she started to run into the house to call for help, but noticed one thing that was very peculiar. His chest was not rising up and down, not even a little. She stood midway between his limp body and the door to her house but got caught in the trance of watching his chest. It remained steady as a board.

She could hear her own heart pumping seemingly as loud as a freight train. Her body was frozen and it seemed her own legs—burning with the sting of the cold water—were cemented to the ground. Each step that she tried to take made her legs feel like boulders. After a few minutes, she realized what a horrible thing she had done.

She never had to use that move in real life; it had only been taught to her in a controlled environment, with Master Choi standing right by her side. She never had to use self-defense, and certainly never in a pool.

Seconds seemed like minutes, and minutes felt like hours. Unlike the horror movies when the murderer-turned-victim comes back to life, Montgomery's body remained still.

She had failed.

Her intent was not to kill. Her attempt to use the sleeper hold as it were intended was futile.

Instead, she involuntarily took it to the next level—the level they warned her to refrain from in her classes.

Montgomery would no longer bother her.

His life had been ended by the hands of the same person who had killed his friend, Shelby. In less than one miserable week, Jacqueline had taken the lives of two people.

Chapter 32: Horrid Decisions

"No, no, don't you dare die on me. This can't be happening. Montgomery Vendora, get the hell up. You came here to kill me. You came to *my* home. Dammit. Get up!" She gained the courage to check for a pulse. "You bastard. You freaking bastard! How dare you?!"

She wanted to kick him and wake him up, but she had waited too long. All rationalization escaped her. She was freezing, soaked, and solely responsible for taking the life of another human being.

But not just any human being. No, that would be too easy. This was just another one of the teenagers that had set her up and were responsible for giving Jacqueline the very first line on her rap sheet. This was the boyfriend of the girl she just killed.

She couldn't think straight. Nothing was making sense. *I can't go to jail. They'll put me away for this. They'll probably reopen the case for Shelby, too, and press charges after all. They'll think I murdered both of them on purpose. He was a murderer, for goodness' sake! Who the hell was this Carmine that he babbled about? Montgomery was right, I did see blood. He murdered a man. Now I murdered him.*

Thoughts spun through her mind like toy horses on a carousel—each one kicking up sand. *This isn't supposed to happen to me. I have goals, dreams, morals! Why can't I just live a normal life?* Her goals glistened before her like the shimmery shadows of a rotating disco ball, only to be destroyed before reaching the dance floor.

By now her hands were freezing and her wet clothes chilled her body to the bone. Confident that no one would walk into her backyard anytime soon, she left the body lying on the cement while she went inside to change into dry clothing.

She looked outside the window, across the street to Ben's house, and contemplated calling him first before ringing the police. If a light had been on, she might have, but the fact that his house was dark meant that he was asleep. She couldn't bring herself to wake him.

Once she was dry and somewhat warmer, she walked back into the kitchen and looked outside. She half expected there to be a vacant space where she had left Montgomery's body, but unfortunately, it was still there.

She leaned against the wall and slid down to the floor of her kitchen staring outside at the person who only moments earlier had tried to kill her. The finality of it all sank in. She shook her head.

I'll go to jail. They'll think I am guilty. They'll think I did this on purpose. Tears streamed down her face. *I can't go to jail.*

She picked up the phone to call Ben. After all, he said she can call any time. Only a moment later, she reconsidered.

I have to leave Ben out of this. I've been nothing but a burden on him since the day we met. I have no choice but to do this on my own.

She stared at her pool and then toward the body of Montgomery Vendora.

I have to get rid of him.

Chapter 33: The End of Innocence

Trepidation and exhaustion, peppered with a generous sprinkle of loathing, empowered Jacqueline to do what needed to be done, even though she didn't want to be the one to do it.

During the course of a lifetime, you may find yourself in a situation beyond your control. Things you swore you would never do, you find yourself doing. The kind of person you loathed is the kind of person you become. Morals that you once held in high regard get thrown off by the wayside. Stress can cause you to do things you otherwise wouldn't do—gruesome things. Like hiding a body.

Okay. I have to analyze this later. For now, I have to move him. By myself! Oh my goodness, but to where? How do you hide a body? Think, Jacqueline!

She only had a few hours before the sun came up and people would be out on the streets. She couldn't possibly move a body in broad daylight.

She rushed into her garage and opened the trunk to her parents' car.

Okay, so how the hell am I going to carry a body all of the way from the backyard into my garage?

Luckily, there was no blood on the body, so at least there would be no visible trace of that. She tried to think back to all of the crime scene investigations that she'd watched on television. If there was anything that could trace his death to her, she would be as good as convicted.

In the corner of the garage, she noticed the utility trolley that her father had given her to move her furniture into her house.

I'm guessing this isn't what my father had in mind, but it'll have to do. She dragged the trolley into the back and positioned it next to the body. Her knees cracked as she bent down to grab Montgomery underneath the arms.

Though he might have weighed no more than one hundred eighty pounds, his limp, wet body felt easily over three hundred.

His body slumped onto the cart and while she knew he was dead, she was careful, as if she could possibly hurt him anymore. His arms flopped over the sides and she neatly positioned them onto his chest. She did so with such precision and ease that it made her nervous. She started second-guessing herself. *Do I actually have the mind of a killer?*

Once she had loaded Montgomery's corpse onto the trolley, she strained every muscle to wheel it in through the kitchen and then back out to the garage.

She was thankful that there was an internal door and did not have to chance it by going into the front yard. She imagined herself struggling as she wheeled out a body, while all of her good-hearted, respectable neighbors watched in awe.

Lifting him into the trunk was not as easy as she had hoped. She had to use all of her strength, positioning part of him on her knee as she glided him over the lip of the trunk. With an extremely loud thump, his lifeless body slammed down inside of the large compartment space.

Her body was trembling. *Well, there's no turning back now.*

She walked into the house to get her keys, still half-expecting Montgomery to rise from the dead and sneak up behind her with the sharpened blade of a shimmery axe. She definitely watched too many late-night horror stories.

Grabbing a coat from her closet, she walked back into the garage and pushed the button for the garage door opener. Trying her best to remain quiet, she opened her car door, climbed in, stuck the keys in the ignition, and backed up onto the desolate street.

She looked toward her new boyfriend's house and wished she could go to him. *I'm sorry, Ben. I put you through too much already. I have to do this. It's the only way.*

As she drove away from her house, she was thankful no one was nearby except for a car halfway down the street. No one would be stalking her anymore. She had taken care of that tonight.

Now what? Drive around aimlessly until I think of where to go? Where is there a remote spot that nobody will see me? Where do people hide dead bodies these days?

Though she watched many movies and documentaries and had read dozens of horror stories—both true crime and fiction—she had never been able to fathom what went through the mind of a murderer. Now, she *was* the murderer. She had no choice but to think like one.

Chapter 34: Bout of Uncertainty

As she drove, the thick fog impaired her vision. She expected to see zombies as she took the next turn.

How fitting. I have a corpse in the trunk of my car and the sky looks like a scene straight out of a Frankenstein movie.

The realization of what she was about to do terrified her. She was becoming increasingly calm and could not believe how simple it all seemed. She was throwing away her life all because she was afraid the police would not believe her. Wasn't that up to fate to decide? Should she be the one taking matters into her own hands?

The more she drove, the more she regretted her decision to dump the body. If she wanted, she could move the body into the backseat and drive straight to the hospital. It may look better in her defense, she reasoned. They may only accuse her of being stupid for moving the body, rather than waiting for professional help. Or, they could slap the cuffs on her right there, accusing her of seeking vengeance for those who framed her years ago. No, she was doing the right thing.

She passed locations that might be remote enough to hide a body, but continued making excuses and thinking of all of the ways that she might get caught. No place seemed good enough.

For the past few days, she had grown accustomed to being fearful, but this was a whole new type of fear, an entirely different experience. Finally, she remembered to breathe.

She envisioned crashing her car, only to wake up in the hospital handcuffed to the metal-framed bed while police officers questioned her about the body in the trunk.

She had to remain calm and focused. There was no room for any mishaps, not even a flat tire.

She passed a wooded area that looked as if it hadn't been walked through in years. It looked perfect, like no one would venture there. That is, until she noticed a small path meant for hikers. It was only a matter of time before they stumbled across the body. *That's not going to work.*

She thought about the dunes of the beach, wondering if she could trek a little bit into the woods and bury him there. Since summer was approaching, however, this did not seem like a viable option.

With each passing mile, Jacqueline became more and more discouraged. Her weary mind kept played tricks on her until she wasn't even remotely convinced that she was going to get away with it.

She was afraid to even look in the mirror, as if she might not recognize the person who stared back at her. Had she changed? Had the events of the past week turned her into a monster? Normal people like her didn't do morbid things like this.

She cringed as she thought of what her sentence would be. Would they take into account the torment Monty had put her through? Could they prove it was self-defense? Who would have thought the fear of getting caught and going to prison was greater than the fear of being continually stalked? People got away with murder all the time, their victims' bodies not found until years later, if at all. Was it because they were seasoned killers, or were they just lucky? Would she have that same luck?

On the left, she passed by a piece of land surrounded by tall trees, plush shrubs, and towering weeds that people used to dump old furniture, tires, curtains, clothes, and other useless items. She couldn't imagine that anyone had ever voluntarily strolled past the first five feet. If she walked a bit further, no one would ever see the body.

She would first dig a hole with the shovel that she had brought and bury the body, the hole hidden under a large piece of furniture. *Yes, this is the place.*

She parked her car and looked around for any bystanders. There were none. She walked through first without the body in order to locate the perfect spot.

As she headed back toward her car to get the body, she stopped dead in her tracks, stiff as a board. She had been so intently focused on finding the ideal burial ground that she had failed to look in her rearview mirror.

If she had, she might have noticed someone following her from a distance. If she had, she might have gotten away with it free and clear. But she had never even stopped to think that another Mr. Crazy could be following her.

Chapter 35: The Stranger

"Howdy, young lady."

"Um, hi."

"What's a young, pretty girl doing out alone on a foggy night like this?"

She froze, as if someone had poured glue on the ground underneath her. She couldn't work out if this person was here to dump something, to arrest her, or had seen a lone girl and had his own perverse thoughts.

She looked at the shovel leaning against the trunk of her car and realized that she made a grave mistake. She shouldn't have taken it out until she was ready. How was she going to explain that? On second thought, if she got to it quickly enough, she could use it as a weapon. "I was just looking for, um...I was just looking to see if there were any hubcaps for my car." He looked at her car, noticing none of them was missing one. "It's for my other car." She had never stuttered a day in her life; yet now, she couldn't finish a word, much less a sentence. Her excuse was lame and she knew it.

"Hubcaps, huh?" He stepped closer and looked at the shovel. "What were you going to use the shovel for?"

"Um, I was just making sure I had room in my trunk." She could only imagine what she must look like. Though she had changed into dry clothes, her hair was still matted to her head from her late-night swim, and no doubt her mascara had run its course down her face. She fumbled with the keys, frantically taking note of her surroundings in case she had to run away. She knew damn well that she wouldn't get far.

"Interesting. So you must think a shovel takes up a lot of room."

"No, um, listen. There's nothing here for me, so I'm going to go." She walked toward her car door, but he walked toward it as well, blocking her hand from reaching the handle. "Listen, sir. I have to go."

"It's the perfect spot, ya know. You shouldn't leave. Finish what you set out to do."

"What?"

"It's the perfect spot. You were smart to choose here."

"The perfect spot, did you say? I'm not quite sure I know what you are talking about, but either way, I really have to go now." She tried to nudge him out of her way, but her attempts were futile. She had barely touched the door handle when he quickly slammed his hands over it. She glanced up at him, fear swimming through her veins like a school of hungry fish.

"I'm quite sure you *do* know *exactly* what I am talking about and I'm telling you, you've done well. This is absolutely perfect."

"Please don't hurt me. I have some money on me. I can get even more money if that is what you want. Please..." She motioned to her purse that she always kept on the passenger seat, before realizing she hadn't brought it with her. How could she when she had a corpse to worry about?

"Hurt you? What type of person do you think that I am? I'm not here to hurt you. In fact, it's quite the opposite. I'm here to help you." Although she wanted nothing more than to believe him, she had to be rational. He wasn't making sense. Why would he be there to help her? "Now, are you going to open the trunk or do I have to do it?"

Jacqueline was dumbfounded; if she stood still, maybe he would walk away. Her keys still dangled loosely from her trembling hands. Looking for the appropriate words, she opened her mouth, but before she could say anything, the stranger grabbed the keys from her and mumbled out loud, clearly aggravated. "I guess I have to do it." He walked over to the trunk and unlocked the latch. "Hiya Montgomery!"

Confused as ever, Jacqueline looked up as if her trance had been broken, biting her nails as if she were still a teen. Finally the words came to her. "You *know* him?"

"Of course I know him. Who the hell do you think I am, the Easter bunny?"

"No, no, but who are you? Are you a cop?" She cringed as she said the words. If he was a cop, then it was game over.

"Do I look like a freaking cop? Yeah, here's my badge." He pointed to an old coffee stain on his white T-shirt.

"I don't understand."

"Listen, I'd love to sit here and shoot the shit with you, but it's quite cold and I don't have a jacket. Unless you would like a hefty jail sentence, help me with this piece of crap and let's get him buried. No one will miss him. It'll be as if he was never here. Poof! And he's gone. Grab me that shovel, will ya? And while you're at it, get the flashlight too. We're going to need it."

Without waiting for her assistance, he grabbed hold of Montgomery's body and threw it over his shoulder like a hefty sack of potatoes.

Jacqueline grabbed the shovel. She was still terrified of whom this man was and what he was capable of, but how much worse could it get? She had already been caught red-handed. Plus, she was here to get a job done and her guest seemed to be hell-bent on helping. Was he a conflicted Good Samaritan? At this point, she didn't care.

With the little energy that she had left, she ran to catch up to him. He had already walked midway through the heavily- polluted field. Once she caught up, she handed him the shovel and he began digging through the earth, dirt piling up in a mound as he swung past his waist. Lucky for them, the ditch had previously been started for one reason or another.

"Looks like someone might've made our jobs easier. I just hope there's not another body down there. Montgomery never did play well with others." The man paused to empty Montgomery's pockets. His soaked jeans were stuck to his body, so it was not so easy to reach in and remove his identification. "I'll get rid of this evidence later." He kicked the body into the hole like he was setting down a pile of old firewood. He landed face up.

Jacqueline cringed as the first few drops of dirt covered the dead man. Since he was still soaked, the dirt caked on him, quickly turning into tiny pockets of mud. It was morbid in every sense of the word, like something straight out of a bad horror flick—only she was the creepy killer instead of the unsuspecting victim. Each time Donovan piled more soil on him, she realized the finality of what she had done. Her fingertips were freezing, yet sweat dripped from her brow.

She had never bothered to close Montgomery's eyelids, so his dead pupils stared directly into hers as the dirt splashed across his face. The conclusiveness of it hit her when all she saw was his pant leg, and then finally, nothing but dirt.

She looked away in the distance and stumbled backwards. Standing at the far field, way past all of the garbage and behind the trees, was a dog with golden mane. From what she could tell, his tail was wagging. Recalling her dreams about the mysterious Butter, she was taken aback. She wanted to go to him. When she wiped her eyes, the dog disappeared as if it had never existed. *Just my mind playing tricks on me. What else is new?*

The burial had taken a bit longer than they had anticipated, but Donovan proved to be thorough. Once the dirt was level with the rest of the landscape, he packed it down and covered it with an old rotting mattress that had been lying right next to it.

She expected a reaction from him, perhaps one of regret, but got nothing in return. He was as cool as a cucumber. His shirt was now soaked from both perspiration and from Monty's wet body dripping onto him, and he was visibly freezing. "That should do it. Cops never come down here. It smells like hell. No one wants to clean it up. I'd venture a guess and say it'll be years before the town ever cleans this up, but...just in case, you can never be too careful." He became winded as he tossed three large, shredded tires over it.

"Now, that should do it. The icing on the cake." Without missing a beat, the strange man began walking back to his truck.

Jacqueline yelled after him. "Wait a minute!" She couldn't comprehend how he was not affected by this.

She looked back over her shoulder to see if the dog truly existed, but nothing was there except for trees, garbage, and a fresh new figment of her imagination. Dismissing it as a fatigue-induced hallucination, she ran to catch up to the man as he ignored her shouts.

He acknowledged her with edginess in his voice. "What? Our work is done here."

"Wait! Is that it? Just walk away?"

"What did you want me to do, say a eulogy over his rotting body? You want to? Go right ahead. I'm not sticking around to get caught. He doesn't deserve that respect, especially after what he had intended for you."

"No, I don't want to give a eulogy, but who are you?"

The man turned around and looked into her eyes with a glazed-over stare. "See that lump of crap we just buried?"

She cleared her throat. She must have breathed in dirt and debris from all of the digging and had a slight tickle. She was also parched. She had been fighting for her life all night without any sleep and hadn't had time to stop for a drink.

"Yes."

"That was Montgomery."

"I know who he was."

"Well, he was a sorry excuse for a human being. He had no morals and didn't care for anyone in this world except for himself. He not only stole from me but was also responsible for singlehandedly killing my partner, who also doubled as Montgomery's boss."

"Carmine?"

"You knew him?"

"No."

"No? It sounds like you knew him."

"Well, Montgomery mentioned him when he also mentioned that I was responsible for killing his girlfriend Shelby, not on purpose, mind you. She was on drugs and passed out in the dead of night. I saw her body at the last minute, but by then, it was too late. Then, to make matters worse, the day Montgomery came over, I saw blood in the truck. I guess that must have been Carmine's?"

"So, *that's* why the piece of crap was after you?"

"I guess. That's what he said when he tried to kill me tonight."

"Makes sense."

"It does?"

"Sure. The cops are turning the heat on full-blast and you were the only missing link to tie Montgomery to the murder. It makes perfect sense that he wanted to make you disappear. I can't say that I blame him, since he wanted to cover his hide. I doubt he cared one iota about his girlfriend though. That was just his way of justifying his actions."

"I guess—if you're a psychopath."

The stranger laughed. "One could argue the fact that you are one as well. After all, only an hour ago you were driving around town with a stiff in your trunk. Do you consider yourself any different than him? You killed him, didn't you? I have one question though. Did you have help or did you do it by yourself?"

"I'm not proud of it! I never hurt anyone in my life—well, not intentionally."

Her mind drifted back to Shelby's lifeless body, and she shooed the thought away. One death was all she could contend with at the moment. "With all due respect sir, I don't even know you. How in the world did you know where I lived? How did you know what *he* was up to?"

"I followed him, which led me to you. I knew he was on some type of a mission. I just didn't know why or what his intentions were. I did know one thing for sure—Montgomery was never up to any good." He shook his head. "So, young lady, you didn't answer my question. Did you do this solo?"

"It's truly none of your business. Why is that so important to you, anyway?"

"Listen, I didn't come here to argue with you. I came here to help, but I could have just as easily contacted the police. You do know that the police station is only about five miles from here, right? I'm sure they could be here within minutes. A hot story like would give them the ability to say they caught Carmine's murderer *and* the person who killed him. This is big news!" Seeing that she was getting more flustered, he toned it down a bit. "I truly do not believe that you are a murderer by nature. As a matter of fact, I'm sure it was self-defense; otherwise I would not be here helping you." While he spoke, she realized she wasn't crying. She almost felt at peace. "When I saw you leave your house without Montgomery, I realized he must be dead—because you were very much alive." She still didn't trust him, but her suspicion had lessened. "Now, he's not my son. Nowhere near it. But, I do feel responsible for his actions, because he was out of control. His whole life was drugs. Same thing with Carmine." Both were shivering. Jacqueline wrapped her arms around her body and noticed his arms had goosebumps as well. His voice quivered. "When it came to the white powder, they both had tunnel vision. They would tell you they were enemies behind each other's back, but wouldn't hesitate to party together during work hours when there were no jobs to do and drugs were available. I guess you can make the argument that I was an enabler. So, I watch him stalk a pretty girl like you and I know he's going to do something. I saw him following you and even saw him try to break into your house. That's when the cops came. I figured they had things under control, but I was dead wrong." She nodded, looking toward the ground, as if that would erase the series of events leading up to now. "I had an advantage over the cops. I know where Monty's stomping grounds are. I knew where to find him. Tonight, I followed him again but almost lost him. I did actually lose sight of him for a while in your neighborhood, but diligently pursued him until I found his car parked around the corner from your house. Don't worry, I've made arrangements to have it moved before anyone even notices."

He was getting edgy and scouting the area. Though he preached that no one visited the dumping ground, she could tell he didn't want to overstay his welcome. "When I got to your house, however, you were already leaving. I was relieved I wasn't too late to save you and that that piece of shit hadn't killed you. You surprised me when you dragged the body into your house and then pulled out of your garage. That could've only meant one thing." The pause was dramatic. "I was also intrigued that you didn't call the cops. That is the part I didn't expect. I didn't see anyone else with you. I thought for sure perhaps a boyfriend helped you do away with Montgomery." She was fidgeting and hoped to leave soon. The situation left her feeling a weird sense of loyalty, like she owed him something for helping her. "Now, to answer *your* question. If there was someone else that helped you kill him, that means someone else knows and someone else can rat us out and get us put in jail for life. I don't want that and I'm pretty sure you don't want that."

It was time for her to interject. "Okay, okay. You've made your point. I understand your concerns. No, there was no one else at my home. No one helped me."

"You killed him all on your own?"

"Yes!"

"And you transported the body to your trunk by yourself?"

"Yes!"

He studied her with curiosity and paused a minute. "Wow. Good job. I'm impressed." He was completely relaxed, using the tone of a father congratulating his daughter for passing a math test.

"Impressed? Are you serious? I killed a man. How is that impressive? Have you done this before?"

"What?"

"You know, kill someone, and hide their body. I mean, are there more down there?"

The man shrugged. "I dunno. Probably. Not from me, though."

"So, this is the first time for you?"

"I don't kiss and tell, um—what's your name?"

She hesitated before answering but realized that he knew where she lived. "Jacqueline."

"Jacqueline. It's really none of *your* business what I do. All that matters is that you are safe. Go home before anyone realizes that you are missing. Dry out your trunk the best that you can and clean your patio, if it is still wet. I don't think the cops will even realize that he's dead and no one will be pestering you for evidence, but…you can never be too careful. The cops probably assume that he skipped down."

"So, you *have* done this before. I don't even know your name."

"The name's Donovan. Pretend you never met me. Think of me as your one-time guardian angel. That lowlife will never terrorize you again. And Jacqueline, don't feel badly about what you did. It was self-defense. He asked for it."

"I don't."

"You don't what?"

She wrapped her arms around her chest as the cool breeze picked up. "I don't feel badly. Not one bit. That's the part that scares me."

She could not help but soften up to Donovan, even though he could quite conceivably be a full-time murderer. They had met under the worst possible circumstances, yet he had a gentle quality with her, like that of a protective father. A human life had been eliminated at her own hands. Together, they had buried a body and he hadn't blinked an eye; yet she felt safe with him and to some degree trusted him.

"You're stronger than I thought, Jacqueline. It shouldn't scare you. You saved your own life. Think of it this way—if you hadn't, it would have been you in that grave—and Montgomery wouldn't have felt any remorse." He motioned toward the dirt that had been thrown over Montgomery's body. "I think you know that. That's why you don't feel bad. Go on. Forget it ever happened. It's over." He looked back one last time. She wasn't comfortable with her actions. Even though she was acting strong, the severity of what she did was going to hit her. Killing someone wasn't something to be taken lightly, she thought, even if it was self-defense. "Jacqueline, there's always going to be a process of elimination—a survival of the fittest, if you will." He looked directly into her eyes, as if he were speaking to her soul. Jacqueline had only met Donovan a few moments ago, but hadn't expected him to be such a philosopher. Listening to him speak changed her impression of him, and even gave her a slightly greater depth of understanding about herself. "What we *choose* to do determines the types of people that we are. Therein lies the difference between each individual." While she had indeed killed Montgomery tonight, in no way did that make her a natural-born killer.

She took a deep breath, analyzing his words, hoping to believe in them. "The cops will look for him for a while to arrest him for Carmine's death, but then the trail will go cold. I checked out his history when we hired him. The apartment is not in his name; the car is not even in his name. There's nothing to go on. Like a feather in the wind, he's gone."

"So, Donovan, if the cops come to my home, do I know him? Do I know you?"

"Well, that all depends. When was the last time you had any interaction with Montgomery?"

"He came to my house to set up a water heater."

"Okay, then sure. Tell the cops the truth about that."

"All right, I guess."

"Good. Take it easy. It's over."

"So, that's really it? You think that it is all over and that it ends here without any repercussions?"

"Of course. Like I told you, no one comes down here, except you."

"And you think we are free and clear."

"I do. Now go home and get some sleep. You look like hell!"

"Sleep. Huh. There's an idea. I guess I should say thank you for your help." Swallowing her pride and her fear, she continued in a whisper. "I don't know that I could have done this on my own."

"Sure you could have, kid. You had the strength, but it might have been a little difficult to lift him and dig the ditch. That ground was still a bit solid. I am glad I met you. Montgomery deserved to die. You did nothing wrong. Remember that. Protecting yourself is not wrong."

"No, but hiding it from the police is."

"Yes, but you would have most likely spent some time in jail and if not, you would have had to at least hire a lawyer. It's over." He got in his car and rolled down the window. "Take care of yourself."

Within seconds, Donovan had sped away. Feeling spooked about being alone in a dumping ground with a corpse, Jacqueline got in her car, started the ignition, and drove off.

Chapter 36: Spring Cleaning

As she continued down the familiar roads, she tried to fathom the unexpected turns that her life had taken within one short week.

The sun was starting to make its initial ascent and she sped home to make sure that she wasn't noticed. Though Donovan had assured her that the police would never be the wiser, she did not quite share his positive outlook.

Could it really be over, just like that? Could she truly just shut her eyes, go to sleep and live a normal, carefree life, or would the night's events change her eternally? What if the unimaginable happened? What if the cops linked his murder to her? Would she crack under pressure? Would she be able to uphold appearances and keep up with the lie? What if they found out? How long would she go to jail for? Would anyone believe her side of the story?

And what would she tell her parents? Would they even believe her? After all, she was responsible for two deaths in one week. It wasn't just two individuals, but two acquaintances from years past who had tried to ruin Jacqueline's life. What would the headlines say? She could picture it now: "Closet Female Killer Strikes Again! News at Eleven."

Did I bring any of this on myself? Was there any possible way that the two deaths were not truly accidents, but something that she had willed to happen? *No, impossible!*

Once she turned the corner to her block, she expected there to be red and blue lights flashing, a roadblock, and the angry, horrified faces of her neighbors as they learned about what happened. To her relief, all she saw when she pulled into the driveway was a rolled-up newspaper that the delivery boy had thrown a few hours earlier.

She pulled into her garage and shut the door behind her before exiting the car. In order to dry out the trunk, she popped the release to let it air out.

She rolled the trolley back into its original location and thought about cleaning it to dispose of any traces of Montgomery. If questioned, she figured that she could always say that he had used it when he was there to install the water heater. She even cleaned the mud off of the shovel and soaked it in a bucket of bleach. She didn't have to be too careful, since Montgomery had been at her house a week earlier for legitimate reasons. There were bound to be fingerprints and hair samples throughout her home; they just shouldn't be anywhere near or in her car.

There was nothing she could do about the tires on her car, but she would have to worry about that later. She threw her sneakers in the garbage, hoping the cops wouldn't be there to search her house before Monday, when the garbage men came to dispose of it.

Her next order of business was to check outside for signs of a struggle. One of her resin chairs had been knocked over, so she set it back into place. Then just to be on the safe side, she hosed down the cement.

Sleep was something she didn't think she was capable of. Her body was still moving as if someone had accidentally pushed the fast-forward button. She had to keep in motion in order to stay sane. She began cleaning like a maniac in order to expunge her negative energy. A psychiatrist's evaluation might report that she was making an attempt to sanitize her soul, rather than her house.

It was now daylight and she knew Ben would be calling her within a few hours. She hoped that she could lie to him without being caught. He was a smart man and extremely intuitive; it was conceivable he would be able to tell that something was up. She loathed the idea of being dishonest, but convinced herself that it did not concern him. She was protecting him. This was new territory for her and she wasn't sure if she could pull it off.

Her body ached, her head throbbed, and she was quickly losing momentum. To her best estimate, she hadn't slept in over twenty-four hours and it might have even been close to forty- eight. The fight that she needed to keep herself alive and the courage required to hide her dirty little secret were both quickly wearing off. While the rest of the neighborhood was just waking up to start the day, Jacqueline lay down on the couch, curled up in a ball, and fell fast asleep.

Chapter 37: Euphoria

She was floating on top of a puffy cloud; her body felt light as a feather. Gravity was nonexistent. She couldn't remember the last time that she had felt completely at ease, as if every muscle had been massaged for hours. It was a euphoric feeling, one that she didn't want to end.

She looked down at her body and was able to notice the tension lines on her face had vanished. She thought she could pass for a teenager. She was youthful.

The past week's troubles were now a distant memory. She could begin her life where she had left off. There were no psychotic stalkers, no plotting murderers, nobody to break into her home in the wee hours of the morning or wander aimlessly around her backyard while she slept only a few feet away. She was free and loved every minute of it.

She saw him run to her and the sight of his floppy, tan ears bouncing with each step brought a wide smile to her face. His visits were always short and always while she was asleep, but she enjoyed them. She had never seen this dog outside of her dreams, except in her imagination, but it was the one thing about sleep she looked forward to.

She had never realized how beautiful the smile of a golden retriever was. There was nothing like it in this world. The back part of Butter's mouth curled up and over, exposing a grin that could melt the hardest of hearts.

She shouted his name. "Butter! You're here. You came to visit."

He jumped into her lap as he always did upon first seeing her, but this time he seemed different. Before, he had always come to her on a mission. But now, he didn't carry the weight of the world. There were no signs of despair shining through his milky brown eyes. There was nothing but pure, unadulterated joy. He was elated.

He dropped his toy-of-the-day into her lap and today, it was a brown squirrel, slobbered on just enough to show that it was one that he cherished.

"Thanks, Butter." She felt the slobber and laughed out loud. He lavished her face with wet puppy kisses and positioned himself right in her lap, where he lay down, content as could be.

This time, instead of rushing off, he was relaxed, calm, and in no particular hurry. After a few minutes, he rolled off her lap and onto his back, exposing his blonde belly for a rub, his eyes closed. Jacqueline took the hint.

When it came time for her to wake, Butter gave her parting kisses and galloped away with the happiest of gaits. As always, a pack of dogs and cats waited in the distance, and he turned back one more time to say good-bye to Jacqueline.

She had a feeling he would be back, and could not wait to see him.

Chapter 38: Cold Case Files

"What do you mean you cannot find him? I asked you to locate his sorry ass fourteen hours ago. How hard is it to track down a vagrant drunk and drug addict?"

"Detective Brown, we looked. We got a warrant for his house, searched inside, went to the local bars and hangouts. Hell, we even searched the alleyways where the rest of the druggies are passed out. No one's seen him. He's flown the coop. He's gone, sir. We tracked credit card usage, but he doesn't have any."

"Of course he doesn't have any! That lowlife doesn't have an ounce of credit to his name. Anything he acquires comes from dirty money or a five-finger discount. The fact that he even held a job for so long still mystifies me. My guess is the only reason he stayed there was because partying was a prerequisite." The officer wasn't quite sure what to do at this point. Detective Brown was still fuming, so he waited to hear the next plan of action. "Dave, go do what you can do to locate this guy. Check the docks, ask around and find out if anyone's seen him. Check the bus stations, stolen cars, relatives, friends—whomever you can contact that knows where this loser lives. My guess is that if he successfully killed Carmine, there were others or will be others. I can't believe I let our prime suspect walk."

"I'm on it, sir. I'll do what I can to find him."

"And then some. We need him in here pronto or the media is going to have a field day with this one."

He was looking in all of the wrong places. Neither of them suspected foul play in the elimination of Montgomery; they assumed he had skipped town, preferring a life on the run to a life in prison.

But there was only so much the force could do to track him down. There were no other murders tied to his record. The only things were burglaries, a few fights, and of course, drugs. Carmine's murder eventually disappeared into the cold case files, and Montgomery's had never even been discovered.

Chapter 39: Second Chances

After the best sleep of her life, Jacqueline woke up feeling refreshed and renewed, like a darkened part of her world had dissipated and been replaced with a sparkling clean slate.

She looked at the display on the clock and couldn't believe it was four in the afternoon. She inspected her house for any signs of evidence that there had been a struggle the previous night. To her chagrin, everything looked as it should. Of course, police forensics could prove otherwise, but she couldn't help but feel relieved that the house was spotless. She only hoped that her conscience would remain the same.

She replayed Donovan's words in her mind. *You saved your own life. If you hadn't, it would have been you in that grave and Montgomery wouldn't have felt any remorse.*

He was right. No matter what anyone said, she did save her own life. She hadn't gone out on a mission to find Montgomery; and if she hadn't had training in martial arts, he would have killed her instead.

She peeked out of her front window; everything was as it should be. The tiny buds on the trees seemed to have turned to little leaves overnight.

When she spotted Ben outside, she walked out to him.

"Hey Jackie! Just in time. Want to get some dinner?"

"Yes, I'm starved!"

"Well, it is four-thirty in the afternoon."

"Yeah, I guess it is."

His tone shifted. "You seem different today. I can't put my finger on it. You seem...happier, more relaxed. I hate to say this, but, given the circumstances of yesterday afternoon, I thought you'd be a little more uptight—not that I'm complaining!"

"No, you're right. I feel much better. I have this premonition that everything is going to be okay after all. I'm just not worried about it anymore. I hate to sound cliché but, what will be will be. I'm prepared now. I'm not going to let some stranger terrorize me."

"Wow. Really? I'm glad to hear it. I like the new Jacqueline."

She smiled. "You know what? So do I, except this has always been me. I've just been in hiding for a little while. I'm back to feeling more in control and trust me, that's a good thing."

"It sure is. You've got the beautiful sparkle back in your eye and that zest that attracted me to you in the first place."

"Thanks, Ben. Thanks for all of your help too."

"Hey, Jacqueline?"

"Yeah?"

"Do you mind if I ask you something? It is probably none of my business, but I just figured I'd ask."

"Sure, anything. What's up?"

"Where did you go at three o'clock in the morning?"

Her face turned white. He saw her. He couldn't know anything, could he?

Think, Jacqueline! Come up with something...fast!

She had no choice. She had to lie. Her mind flashed back to Montgomery's burial ground and to the strange but helpful interaction with Donovan. She recalled his words. He was right. She had to remember that.

As she looked up at Ben, she wanted to tell him. Her heart ached that she was going to lie to him, but she had to do it. Montgomery was dead. There was no reason to harp on it any longer. "Oh, well, I couldn't sleep, so I went for a ride and then stopped at the pharmacy for a sleep aid. Hence the reason I slept so well!"

"Okay, I thought something was wrong. Glad it was nothing."

She just smiled and brushed it off. Her dirty little secret was still safe. He didn't know anything and there was no reason for him to know anything. Like Donovan had said, it was over.

Chapter 40: Tainted Hope

Just as they finished talking, she saw the reflection of the lights flashing behind her. Her heart sunk. They were coming after her.

This was it. They were going to arrest her. They had found the body. The fear of going to jail far surpassed her recent fears of being murdered. Who would have thought jail was worse?

She looked toward the house that she had made into a home and imagined the devastated expression on her parents' faces when they discovered what their daughter had done.

She tried to remain calm, keeping Donovan's instructions playing in her head. *Go on. Forget this ever happened. It's over. The cops will look for him for a while to arrest him for Carmine's death, but then the trail will go cold. I checked out his history when we hired him. The apartment is not in his name; the car is not even his. There's nothing to go on. Like a feather in the wind, he's gone.*

Ben looked up and noticed the two police cars that had pulled up beside them. Jacqueline's eyes pleaded with him, although he didn't see and wouldn't know why.

Ben's voice woke her out of her trance. "Good evening, officers!"

"Evening, sir. We're looking for a young boy, six years old. His mother said he was playing in the street and disappeared over two hours ago. They live around the corner. He was wearing a yellow shirt. Either of you seen him?"

The mother of the child was frantic, yelling out his name a few blocks down. They caught site of her amid a group of people. Her desperate screams echoed through the crowd. "Tommy!"

Jacqueline couldn't help but exhale and relax her shoulders. She was happy they weren't after her, but immediately felt for the mother of this small child.

Just as she started to look around her, another police car came from the opposite direction and pulled up next to them. In the front seat sat a young boy. The officer rolled down his window and yelled across to the other police car. "We got him. I'm taking him to his mom. He was playing in the old tree house down the road. He's okay. Scared, but okay."

The squad car zipped off in the direction of his mother and once they reached her, the little boy jumped out and into the arms of his loving mother. "Thanks for your help!" she called.

Once again, Ben and Jacqueline were alone. Jacqueline's face was still bone-white.

"You okay?"

"Yes, just a little spooked. I thought we were going to find the remains of a little boy. I'm fine." She steadied her legs and prayed that the rest of her life would not be plagued by this same paranoia. "So, you were asking me about dinner? What did you have in mind, Ben?"

"If you're ready to, I say we hit that new Chinese restaurant that just opened up."

"Ready as I'll ever be!"

On the ride over, they talked and laughed as though the weight of the world had been lifted.

Donovan might be right, she thought. Perhaps not too much effort will be expended in locating Montgomery. Even if they did search, they would never suspect Jacqueline. If anything, they would investigate the usual suspects in the local drug and crime scene. Jacqueline was finally starting to believe that she was safely out of harm's way.

Chapter 41: Peanut Butter

As they walked into Fusion's, they were seated next to a couple that Jacqueline immediately recognized. "Mr. and Mrs. Palmer! What a surprise seeing you here!"

Ben recognized them as well. "Hello my ex-neighbors! How are you doing?"

"Hi Jacqueline. Hello Ben!" Mr. Palmer stood up to shake their hands, while Mrs. Palmer gave each of them a kiss on the cheek.

"What's new in the old neighborhood?" Mrs. Palmer was the chatty one. Her husband sat back down and continued with his meal, smiling every so often to demonstrate he was listening. His wife sat next to him. "Why don't you sit with us? It'll give us a chance to catch up, and then I don't have to listen to Charlie drone on and on." She winked at Jacqueline with a sly smile on her face. Charlie gave his wife a loving pinch.

"Not much. We had a bit of excitement today when a little boy went missing. The cops were combing the neighborhood, but they found him unharmed, thankfully. Other than that, it's been quiet."

"We are so happy we have you as our tenant. How do you like the house, Jackie?"

"I love it. It's quaint and just what I need."

"Oh good!" she exclaimed. "We always loved that house. We wouldn't have moved, except for Charlie here wanted a home on the beach. I have to say I don't mind it, either. It's refreshing."

Mrs. Palmer's next words hung in midair like a hot air balloon on a summer's day. "I hope that little Butter hasn't been bothering you!"

Jacqueline almost fell out of her seat. "I'm sorry, who?"

"Miriam! Stop pestering people about him. Let him rest in peace!"

"Charlie, I'm just teasing. I'm sure she knows that, don't ya, Jackie?

While the couple was bickering back and forth, she tried to understand what was happening. "I'm sorry, whom did you say?"

The husband spoke this time, exasperated, but with a softened tone. "Butter. He was our beloved golden retriever. He passed away a few years ago. God, how we loved that dog. Such an angel."

The wife now interjected. "The entire neighborhood loved him. You remember him, don't you, Ben?"

"Sure do! Butter used to sneak over to my house every Sunday, and he and I would share a bagel, lightly toasted with cream cheese. He always sneaked back home before you even realized he was missing!"

"So that's how he gained so much weight!"

"Yeah, and you were blaming me, Miriam. You can apologize at any time."

"Oh, not a chance. You sneaked him snacks under the table all of the time. How do you think he got his name?"

"I'm sorry. Butter was your dog?" Jacqueline was the only one not participating in the banter, confusion painted on her face like a fluorescent tattoo.

"Yes, honey. He was truly one of our own. We loved him more than most people love their own children!"

"So, don't keep us in suspense. How did he get his name?" Ben was egging them on.

"When we first got him, he was a scrawny little thing. We had rescued him from a shelter. There were eight in the litter. Two had died. Purebred golden retrievers. Can you imagine? But no one wanted them. The breeder was going to let them die because they had parvovirus. People like that should go to jail, as far as I'm concerned. Thankfully, a nice woman from the shelter picked them up and immediately provided them with medical attention. She came along just in time. When they were well enough to be adopted, we instantly fell in love with Butter."

"Right, except his name was Wilbur, like the pig."

"Do you want to tell the story or shall I, Charlie?"

"Oh, by all means!" The couple consistently bickered, but it was plain to see that they were fooling around. "So, like I was saying, we brought him into our home and from day one, we knew he was special. I could swear, sometimes it was like that dog was psychic. Isn't that right, Charlie?"

"Yep. That dog damn near scared me sometimes. If he wasn't such a lovable dog, I'd be a little afraid."

"He used to come running out of the room when we were looking for him, before we even had a chance to call him, and then carry things in his mouth and deliver them to us. Things that we were looking for only moments earlier. It was as if he knew."

Each one kept interrupting the other. Charlie was the next to boast. "He couldn't have enough toys—especially his cherished tennis ball. We had to get him a collar and attach the tennis balls to it by a rubber ribbon so that he wouldn't lose it. Once the ball broke, we had to tie another on. He carried that thing with him everywhere."

"We only found out *after* he died that he'd venture out on his own, when we weren't looking. Somehow, he always got out, presumably by the back gate, but he actually looked both ways before crossing the street. At least now we know *why* he ventured out—free bagels." Miriam faked an angry look toward Ben. "I suppose it was a good thing because when we got him, he needed to gain a bit of weight. He ate his food without any issues, so we were lucky there. We had to give him supplements too, but he wasn't having it, so Charlie had a bright idea to stick the pill in peanut butter." Her husband was now laughing as his wife continued. "From the moment he twisted the lid off the jar, Butter behaved like a different dog, although typically he acted more like a person. He'd jump into Charlie's lap and I kid you not, stuff his snout in the jar. He was way too fast for us to stop him. When he lifted his face out of it, he had peanut butter stuck to his snout, his whiskers and somehow in his eyelashes, but he did not mind one bit. His tail couldn't have wagged any faster. This was the real thing. Peanut Butter.

"And, that's how he got his name," she finished. "All of his records say Peanut Butter, but we called him Butter for short." Jacqueline took this all in, recalling the intelligent golden retriever in her dreams with the tennis ball dangling around his collar. She had to pinch herself to make sure that she was awake now. Had she ever seen a picture of their dog? She tried to remember if they had ever spoken about this before. "What's wrong, honey? You look like you've seen a ghost. I hope my story of Butter isn't upsetting you."

"Oh, no. Not at all. It's delightful, actually. So, tell me, what happened to Butter?"

"He passed away a few years ago. His legs gave out and the arthritis was quite bothersome. He couldn't even get up anymore. We didn't want to, but we had to put him to sleep. We could not let him suffer any longer. Charlie wanted to bury him in the backyard."

"And did you?" Jacqueline spoke a little too soon, as if her life depended on the answer.

"No," said Charlie. "We had him cremated."

"Oh!"

"But Miriam decided to scatter his ashes in the backyard and at the beach—two places he loved the most. She swears he used to come to her in her dreams. Is that the craziest thing you have ever heard?"

As she ran her fingers through her hair—a nervous habit she picked up when she was young—Jacqueline answered with a slight chuckle. "Wow, yeah. I mean that would be something, huh? If your dog could come to you in your dreams?" She knew she looked distracted.

"Trust me, he has. I've even woken up to dog hair on the blankets, and we haven't adopted another dog...yet. He's always trying to tell me something, either to warn me or approve. I'm telling you, I know it sounds crazy, but Butter is still here." Miriam waved her hands through the air.

"I believe it." More than anything, she wanted to share her experiences with Miriam. In her dreams, Butter had been trying to warn Jacqueline, but she hadn't realized that the dangers he had warned her about were real.

Chapter 42: Sweet Dreams

After mulling it over for a few minutes, Jacqueline decided to take a risk and come clean. "I have to admit something." She had the full attention of the table. All eyes were upon her and she wished she hadn't opened her mouth, but it was too late.

"I've had a few dreams lately and amazingly enough, there was a golden retriever in them. It sounds like a lie, but I swear it's the truth. The dog was named Butter. His name was printed on a peanut-shaped dog tag. Did he happen to have a tag that looked like that?"

"No! He had a standard dog tag—one that looks like a bone—but, it makes perfect sense. A peanut-shaped tag? 'Butter' written on it? Peanut Butter! That had to be him!"

Ben looked at Jackie and softened up a bit. He felt like perhaps she was fooling with the Palmers and hoped that she wasn't. That would be cruel, even if she was joking.

"Jackie, have you really?"

"Yes! I swear it. I never said anything because I thought it was only a dream with no relevance, but he was there, and more than once."

Miriam and Charlie studied her, trying to ascertain if she was telling the truth or pulling their leg. Jacqueline sensed their uncertainty. In almost a whisper, she spoke to Miriam first. "I'm sorry if I upset you, but it is true." Shaking her head, she said, "Perhaps it is a coincidence. Just one of those things."

Miriam interrupted with tears in her eyes. "I believe you, Jackie. I'm not angry with you. Up until this point, I thought it was my mind playing tricks on me, but he's still here. He's still trying to finish his work here on Earth.

Dreams are the only way he can come to us. How was he? Was he warning you about anything?"

Jackie looked toward Ben and nodded. In every dream where Butter had showed up, danger had been sure to follow— all but the very last dream she had had of him. He had been completely at ease then.

She decided to at least tell half the truth, without bringing up the incident in the pool. She had to remember to keep the story in present tense. "There has been someone following me, I guess some type of stalker, for the past week."

"Oh my gosh, Jackie!"

"It's okay." She looked to Ben and held his hand for comfort. "We're working on resolving it; however, Butter came to me while I was sleeping. I never really paid attention to his signals. I thought he was a goofy golden retriever who invaded my sleep. I never realized the relevance."

Tears streamed down Miriam's face. "He was always a goofball."

"I'm so sorry. Should I go on?"

"Yes, please." Charlie was the one to speak now, apparently enthralled. Though he seemed to still be in disbelief, he didn't poke holes in her story.

"Anyway, he came out of nowhere and left almost as quickly as he arrived. Every time, he ran toward a pack of dogs and glanced back at me before leaving."

Miriam nodded. "The Rainbow Bridge."

"What?" Never having owned a dog, Jacqueline had no clue what she was speaking about.

"The Rainbow Bridge. You never heard of it?"

"I'm sorry, no."

"Ever have a pet?"

"No, not really. I had a hamster once, but that was it."

Miriam looked through her purse and handed a folded-up piece of paper to Jackie. "Read it and you'll understand."

Once Jackie had finished, she, too, was crying. She now understood the dream and all of the warnings Butter had been giving her. She comprehended why he had always left the way that he had and why all of the dogs and cats had been waiting for him. Her dream was real. And so was Butter.

Ben broke the solemn silence and looked at Jacqueline in a new light. He hadn't known of the dream but seemed amazed by its intensity.

The waiter came just in time to place their orders and lighten the mood. While the two couples waited for their food, they relaxed, talked, and even had a few laughs.

But it went without saying that a peculiar bond had formed between them. Once their evening ended, they hugged good-bye. The relationship had transitioned from that of neighbors and landlords to that of friends.

"Some evening, huh?" commented Ben. "I never knew you were having those dreams. That's amazing."

"It truly is. I never thought anything of them, but all I can say is that Butter did exist and he did try to warn me. Last night he came to me again with no warning signals whatsoever. He was fun, loving, and completely at ease. Because of that dream, I was relaxed today and couldn't help but feel that the worst of my issues were over." Ben watched as Jacqueline smiled. "Now I know they are."

Epilogue

After Ben and Jacqueline left the restaurant, they stopped at a park to take a walk.

Midway into their walk, they noticed a rather large, muscular man screaming at a golden retriever pup that had to be no more than two years old.

"When I say come, you come! Do you hear me?"

They arrived just in time to see the pup cower to the ground, clearly terrified of its master. It seemed the more the dog displayed fear, the louder its owner screamed.

"Now you want to listen, huh? You stupid dog!" He yanked on the leash hard enough to make the dog yelp in obvious pain. From what she could see, the frightened dog's hair was matted and it appeared undernourished.

Jacqueline couldn't stand it anymore and raced toward the man and the dog.

"Sir, I couldn't help but notice that you and your pup are having some difficulty." She really wanted to say how she couldn't help but notice what an imbecile he was, but thought it was wiser to use a mellow approach. She pictured wrapping the collar around his neck and pulling just as hard, but stored her violent thoughts safely away. Apparently she didn't know her own strength these days.

"Yeah, so? What business is that of yours?"

Ben stood closely behind, shocked at Jacqueline's sudden plan of action, but ready to defend should the situation arise.

"Well, it's not my business, really, however, my nephew just lost his dog," she lied, "and if you'd like I can take your dog off of your hands."

"What makes you think I don't want my dog? Look how obedient he is." He pulled on the leash once again, forcing the dog to sit upright, his back legs shivering, noticeably afraid.

She didn't even know where she was going with this. She hadn't considered adopting a dog and had no idea what she was in for. Her thoughts flashed back to the dog in her dream and the only thing that she knew for certain was that she wanted to take this pup as far away from his owner as possible. She only had a minute to perfect her charm.

"Well, it's just that you didn't look all too happy. Listen, how much would you want for him?"

Ben's eyes widened. Was she really going to buy this dog? Each day that he spent with her was a fascinating learning experience.

The man laughed. "You want to buy this mutt? Look at him. He doesn't listen. He's dumb as a rock. I feed him and give him a place to stay and this is what I get in return. The quivering fool."

Her patience was wearing thin, but she was getting through to him.

"That's okay, sir. I'd be happy to take him off of your hands." Trying not to sound desperate, she said a silent prayer that he would concede.

Realizing he could make money, he laughed a gruff sounding cackle. "Give me a hundred. No, you know what, give me two hundred. Gotta explain to the wife why I don't have no dog."

Jacqueline looked at his left hand. Just as she thought—no wedding ring. She doubted anyone would marry this buffoon.

As she reached in her purse, she realized she was fifty dollars short. Her heart sunk, but within seconds, Ben handed her a crisp fifty dollar bill.

"Two hundred dollars sir. Here ya go, please hand me the dog."

With one last tug, the man yanked on the leash before handing it to Jacqueline. To her, it felt as if she had just been handed a precious diamond and held on tightly to the handle. Before the man walked away, she had to ask. "What's his name?"

"His name? His name is Useless." With that he laughed as he fanned his money and walked away.

Ben stared at her half smirking and half in curiosity. He noticed a fierce, determined look in her eyes like she was ready to kill.

She confirmed it for him. "Never in my life had I wanted to hurt someone so badly. I'm furious!"

"I can tell! What kind of man treats a defenseless animal that way? The dog is starving. You can see his ribs. What are you going to do with him?"

Trying to recover from her rage, she looked at the innocent pup wagging his tail at her feet. She considered bringing him a shelter and then realized she didn't have the heart.

"I haven't come to a conclusion yet, actually. I just wanted him out of that man's grasp. But, I think I'll keep him. It will be nice to have someone there to keep me sane. I only hope I know what I'm doing." She bent down to hug the retriever who welcomed the embrace without cowering one bit. Ben knelt down as well as the dog rolled over looking for a much needed belly rub, trusting his new friends immediately.

"Don't worry, Jackie. I'll be there to help you with him. I know a thing or two about dogs. You'll be just fine. He trusts you already."

"Really? Well, that's a pretty strong commitment."

"I can handle it if you can."

She had to laugh. He was good. "I can't tell you how relieved I am to hear that. Let's get out of here before that evil man changes his mind and comes back."

As they hurried to the car, the retriever never looked back for his previous owner, and happily frolicked through the park with his new friends. He focused his attention on a rabbit that scurried across his path.

"Have you thought of a name, Jackie?"

"Yeah, I think it's one that fits him perfectly." She watched the dog's eyes stalk the rabbit. "I'm going to call him Elmer."

ALSO WRITTEN BY ELIZABETH PARKER:
Finally Home

"There is a time in everyone's life where they have been emotionally inspired or amazed by something that was completely unexpected. Sometimes it is so touching, that they want to share their experience with the world and tell their story.

This particular story is about a precious heart along with a free-spirited little boy who owns that heart. This little boy has expressive brown eyes, a beautiful smile, and golden brown coat that he never takes off. He also has a huge pinkish-brown nose and four very fast legs. His name is Buddy. He answers to that...when he wants to."

Buddy was a dog that no one wanted, yet he became one of the quirkiest, friendliest, smartest and most cherished of dogs. The reader is not only drawn into the book, but learns from the unfortunate mistakes of others and how to think outside of the proverbial box. It gives the reader hope that if they are going through a similar ordeal, they can also successfully overcome any related obstacle.

If you are looking for a great gift for both dog lovers and even non-dog lovers, this book is perfect. Get ready to laugh a little and perhaps even shed a few tears.

A portion of the proceeds from the sale of "Finally Home" will be donated to an animal rescue group.

Final Journey: Buddys' Book

After the publication of "Finally Home," Buddy was diagnosed with terminal cancer. Once the unthinkable happened and Buddy's precious life was cut short, his family was left heartbroken and devastated.

At the same time, in another state, poor economic conditions forced another family to give up their golden retriever.

As fate would have it, his name...was Buddy.

While they were mourning the loss of their beloved dog, another dog was mourning the loss of his treasured family.

Brought together by misfortune, they entered each other's lives to help put back together the pieces of their broken hearts.

This story is for both Buddys, producing the subtitle "Buddys' Book."

*A portion of the proceeds from the sale of this book will be donated to an animal rescue organization.

Phobia

Growing up with phobias that have terrified him his entire life, Matt Brewer had finally made the decision to go to counseling, seeking help once and for all.

He entrusted his emotions in the hands of strangers and depended on them to help conquer his fear. What he did not count on was having his fears become a distinct reality, leaving him fighting for his life and the lives of those around him, including his girlfriend whom he intended to marry.

Tortured and bound, he comes face to face with evil with no one to hear his screams. Time is of the essence and it's a literal race against the clock in order to make it out alive.

*A portion of the proceeds from the sale of this book will be donated to a dog rescue organization.

Unwanted Dreams

What if the life you were living was not the one you were meant to live?

One man. One moment in time. One horrific night. That was all it took.

Alexandra had married the man of her dreams and they had their whole life ahead of them. They had a wonderful marriage, a beautiful house and essentially they could not be happier. Things were falling into place as intended, until one beautiful evening turned devastatingly tragic.

The catastrophic events that transpired ensured that none of their lives would ever be the same. Faced with an impossible moral decision, Alex had to make a choice that would come back to haunt her in years to come, once again forcing her to tempt the hands of fate.

How does a random murder shatter the many lives of those within the killer's path? How do you pick up the pieces of your life when unforeseen circumstances alter your future forever?

Unwanted Dreams provides just the right amount of twists and turns, leaving the reader in suspense, pondering the following question: How strong is the bond that exists between families and how far would you be willing to go to save your own?

*A portion of the proceeds from the sale of this book will be donated to a dog rescue organization.

Evil's Door

Childhood rumors are often prevalent in a family-oriented community. Some boast that they have seen a UFO flying overhead while others claim to have witnessed a ghost soaring through the trees. Some stories are so believable that they trickle down from sibling to sibling, friend to friend; creating a neighborhood buzz that lingers for years.

Ryan Sheffield's neighborhood was no different. Though no one would admit it, adults and children alike were freaked out by the eccentric woman who lived in the ghastly corner house, but aside from that, his world as he knew it was an ordinary one.

Bizarre situations did not surface until Ryan began working at his very first job. To his peers and superiors, it was just a traditional office. To Ryan, it was much more than that after a series of inexplicable occurrences haunted his every conscious moment.

Through a bit of intense research, he uncovered the building's gruesome history and was led down its horrifying path. He opened the door to a hell he did not want to live in and tried his best to avoid the evil that surrounded him. The truth revealed itself to him in more ways than one; a truth he was better off not knowing and one that could essentially end his life.

*A portion of the proceeds from the sale of this book will be donated to an animal rescue organization.

Bark Out Loud!

"Bark Out Loud" is a compilation of motivational and thought-provoking quotes—some about dogs and some about life in general—that have been inspired by my own dogs, as well as those that I've met and those that I'll never have the opportunity to meet. Many of the quotes are meant to motivate, some are meant to initiate a smile and others are simply thoughts to ponder. All of the animal-related pictures in this book are either of dogs or cats that we—or someone we know— had the opportunity to rescue. If you enjoy goofy photographs of animals or pretty landscape pictures along with uplifting words, then this book is for you!

A portion of the proceeds will be donated to animal rescue organizations.

*Please note this is a short book under fifty pages.

My Dog Does That!

Are you a dog-lover? If so, you're not alone!

My Dog Does That! is a humorous, uplifting, feel-good book about what all dog-lovers have in common: dogs and the reasons that we love them.

Some days they make us laugh, other days they make us crazy, but one thing is for certain; they do some interesting things that non dog-lovers wouldn't understand.

Do you ever feel a bit awkward due to the stunts that your dog has pulled? Do you ever feel as if you are the only one whose dog embarrasses them at not-so-convenient times? How about those wonderfully sweet and tender moments that you so badly want to brag about, but are afraid others may not understand?

We dog-lovers can all relate to the everyday occurrences when it comes to our furry friends because our dogs do that too!

Made in the USA
San Bernardino, CA
08 December 2014